VIRIDIAN
VENUS ANGEL

First published 2013 by A & C Black,
an imprint of Bloomsbury Publishing Plc
50 Bedford Square
London WC1B 3DP

www.bloomsbury.com

ISBN 978-1-4081-8611-4

A CIP catalogue for this book is available from the British Library.

Printed and Bound by CPI Group (UK) Ltd, Croydon CR0 4YY

1 3 5 7 9 10 8 6 4 2

MIX
Paper from
responsible sources
FSC® C020471

SUSAN GATES

VIRIDIAN
VENUS ANGEL

QUICKSILVER

CHAPTER ONE

People were disappearing from the streets of Franklin.

It wasn't like the town didn't have enough problems. Most people were now cured of the plant virus that had infected humans. But things weren't back to normal, not by a long way.

Jay Rainbird listened as his dad and Dr Moran discussed Franklin's missing citizens.

They were in the basement of Franklin High, Jay's old school. It was here that Dr Moran and a few Immunes had hidden out and found a cure for the plant virus.

Dr Moran was a hero now. He'd saved mankind, changed Verdans back into humans. Even Jay's dad, who wasn't easy to impress, wouldn't say a bad word about him.

But I say you're a cold-hearted creep, Jay was thinking, glaring at Dr Moran. *And I'm never, ever going to say different.* He considered that. *Well, maybe I will when we get Toni back. But maybe not even then.*

In Jay's opinion, Dr Moran had abandoned Toni. He'd been too busy saving the world to rescue his own daughter when she'd been captured by Viridian and his warriors to be turned into a human/plant mutant, freakier by far than any Verdan.

And Verdans were freaky enough, thought Jay, with their green chlorophyll skin, and creepy green eyes, and green teeth, like the undead, in horror films.

'Yes, but can we take these reports *seriously*?' Dr Moran was saying. 'That people are disappearing from our streets? Have we got any actual *proof*?'

Jay's dad shrugged. 'Just what people say.'

'Society's still in chaos after the plant virus,' Dr Moran pointed out. 'Families got broken up. Every family's missing someone.'

Dad nodded. When people got the virus, turned into plant/human hybrids, they didn't care about family or friends any more. They only cared about their own survival. They wandered off alone, looking for water and the sunniest places. But now people were being cured, families wanted to get back together. There were photos of missing loved ones pinned up all over town. They all had sad, desperate messages underneath. Like, 'THIS IS OUR DAUGHTER AMY. SHE'S ONLY SIX YEARS OLD. IF YOU SEE HER, PLEASE, PLEASE, BRING HER HOME!!'

'Yeah, I know there are still people missing,' frowned Dad. 'But this is different. This is people who are cured, back with their families. And then just vanishing again, into thin air.'

Jay didn't care about those people. He was on fire with frustration and he couldn't stay quiet a second longer. 'What about Toni?' he burst out, furiously. 'When are we going to look for her? You've promised me every day, "We'll go tomorrow." And it's been four weeks now!'

Four weeks since he'd seen Toni fly off into the night sky. She'd still had the plant virus, still been a Verdan. But worse than that, she'd been a victim of extreme experiments. She'd become a Venus Angel, with wings grafted onto her back on the orders of Viridian, the Verdans' Supreme Commander.

But now Viridian was dead, infected with the black spot fungus that had killed him and his Immune Hunters. The last time Jay saw the power-mad monster, his massive body was putrefying. His glossy green skin was being eaten by black mould. Fungus spores were puffing from his mouth and nostrils.

But you didn't actually see his dead body, did you? said a tiny, nagging voice in Jay's head.

Yeah but that's 'cos he crawled away to die somewhere, Jay reassured himself. *Anyway, stop thinking about him. He's history.*

Those days of terror, when Viridian kept order using his fearsome Immune Hunters, were dead and buried.

'So when are we going to find Toni?' Jay demanded again.

But Dr Moran had turned his back, like he'd already dismissed the question. He strode off towards his laboratory in another part of the basement.

Now Jay was alone with Dad, his anger and bitterness boiled over. 'Why are you on Dr Moran's side? He doesn't care about Toni. You should be on *my* side. You *promised* me we'd find her!'

Dad looked guilty and Jay knew why. It was because Dad had a habit of breaking promises, long before the virus. He'd tell Jay, 'I'm back for good this time.' Then he'd take off somewhere, for months, even years, leaving Jay to be raised by Gran.

Jay had thought that Dad had changed. That fighting against Viridian's evil empire had brought them closer together, given them new respect for each other.

But it seemed to Jay, at that moment, like Dad was going back to his bad old ways.

'If you won't come with me,' threatened Jay, 'I'm going on my own. Why do I need you? You were never around when I needed you anyway.'

'Yeah, I was,' protested Dad. 'What about when I found you, after Toni got captured and Viridian almost killed you? When we hid out down the mine? You were in really bad shape.'

But Jay wasn't in the mood to listen to reason.

He watched Dad, running his hands up and down his wiry, tattooed arms. Jay knew Dad only did that when he felt under pressure.

'You can't go on your own,' Dad went on. 'Communications are still down. It's crazy out there.

8

Everyone's trying to take control. Some Verdans won't change back and human vigilante groups are hunting *them* down. They even say some of Viridian's Immune Hunters didn't die from the fungus. That those green freaks are roaming out there in the woods...'

Jay shivered. Immune Hunters, with their vicious grafted-on plant weapons – poison spines, cruel hooks, strangling vines – hated humans like poison. Those psychos had nearly killed him and Toni more than once, before Toni turned Verdan.

She was one of them now, a mutant warrior, with plant weapons of her own. Did she hate humans too?

No way, Jay told himself. *She won't hate me, anyhow.*

'And then there's the dogs,' Dad was saying. 'The pet dogs the Verdans didn't want any more. They've gone feral. They're hunting in packs in the woods...'

'I don't care!' Jay interrupted wildly. 'I don't care what's out there. Immune Hunters, dogs, vigilantes, so what? I *promised* Toni when she flew away. I promised her, "I'll come and find you." And who else is going to do it? Her own dad doesn't care.'

Dad's voice became gentler. 'Look son,' he said. 'It's not that he doesn't care. He just thinks she won't care about *him*. That she doesn't want to be cured. He says she's so far from human now, it's cruel to try. Best to leave her like she is.'

'Cruel? What's he talking about? That's total crap!'

'But he offered her the cure, didn't he? Just before she flew off? You saw her. She smashed the vaccine bottle out of his hand.'

'She'll care about *me*,' Jay shouted, his voice getting louder and angrier, to drown out his own doubts. 'They forced her to be a Venus Angel, put those wings on her back. She wants to be like she was before. She wants to be with *me*.'

It seemed to Jay that Dad was itching to say something. But, in the end, he didn't.

'Anyway, I'm going, right?' Jay told him.' And nothing's going to stop me. I promised Toni. And I keep my promises.'

Jay didn't add, 'Not like you.' But he didn't need to. He knew Dad had got the message because if he rubbed at those tattoos any harder he'd rub them clean away.

Finally Dad spoke. 'All right, we'll go tomorrow. Me and you. Now will you calm down? But I'm telling you, Jay, nothing can be like it was before. Nothing. Not even you and Toni, not even after she's cured.'

Jay ignored that last sentence. Instead, he stared at Dad, in silence, for a long, long time. Finally he said, his eyes full of suspicion, 'You really mean it? We're *really* going tomorrow?'

'I said so, didn't I?' said Dad.

'OK, OK, don't get mad,' said Jay. 'That's great, Dad.' He went running towards the lab. It was the first time for weeks that he'd felt happy. 'I'm going to get vaccine from Dr Moran, so we can take it with us.'

'Just don't tell him what it's for,' warned Dad. 'Like I said, he thinks maybe Toni should be left where she is.'

'That's such crap,' said Jay. 'This is how it will be. Right? When we get Toni home she takes the cure. Then she has surgery, gets those freaky wings cut off her back. Then she'll be normal again, won't she? And she'll be really grateful to us.'

CHAPTER TWO

Toni was in the swamplands, south of Franklin. Since she'd flown away from Jay and her dad, watched them become as small as ants below her, she hadn't seen a single human being. No-one, not even Verdans, came to these quaking bogs, where carnivorous plants thrived. But, to a Venus Angel, it felt like coming home.

Toni crouched among pitcher plants, rising around her a metre high. From inside their traps, tall slender trumpets, she could hear the frantic whine of flies. They'd crawled in and couldn't climb back up the slippery walls. Now they were being digested, slowly.

All the predator plants around her had caught something. Tiny sundew plants had gnats struggling in their sticky tentacles. Venus fly traps, miniature versions of her own wings, had their leaves clamped shut, like clam shells. Inside them were buzzing flies, being slowly drained dry of body fluids.

Toni watched them fondly, as if they were her subjects, in her own personal kingdom.

'Good hunting,' she told them, smiling.

She still used English, to think and talk to herself, sometimes. But her human speech was getting rusty. It belonged to that other world she'd lived in before she became a Venus Angel and had to learn a whole new set of skills to survive.

But she still thought about that boy sometimes. What was his name?

'Jay,' Toni said out loud. Her own voice seemed strange, as if it belonged to someone else. She said 'Jay' again, just to reassure herself that the sound was coming out of her own mouth.

In her mind, she suddenly saw him, far below her, heard his frantic cry: *I'll come and find you. I promise!*

Then a screech came from above. Toni looked up. She forgot about Jay. A hawk came streaking in from the west. Bam! It hit a pigeon in the air above her. There was an explosion of feathers and the hawk spiralled off, the pigeon grasped in its talons. Its harsh wild cries faded into the distance.

Toni's green lips curved into a grin. She'd learned a lot from hawks.

'You were useless at flying before,' she told herself.

But now she was getting better. Better at flying and hunting. Like the hawk, she snatched birds to eat out of the air now, sometimes squirrels from trees. Her wings snapped shut in a tenth of a second.

She opened her glossy, green wings. Bones and grey fur fell out in a neat, dry package. Her wings were blood red inside, rich with nutrients from the squirrel she'd just finished digesting. They had spines round the edge to stop prey escaping. She took all her meals through her wings now. She'd stopped eating by mouth completely. It was as though she'd forgotten how.

She spread her gorgeous wings wide, to soak up the sun. Her green neck twisted, like a plant stem, so her face could bask in its rays. She stayed like that, totally still, for ages, half gargoyle, half beautiful stone angel.

'Time to fly,' Toni told herself at last.

She took off in a crimson green blur, fluttering her wings like a great butterfly. Little birds flew up from the swamplands and mobbed her. Like the hawks, lords of the skies before she came along, Toni ignored them.

'Higher,' Toni told herself, her green eyes, fierce as an eagle's, staring straight at the sun.

She loved flying. It was perfect freedom.

She never wanted to be human again. She would have felt sorry for them, poor pathetic wingless creatures. But plant/human hybrids don't feel pity. Or love, or even the need for friendship.

She soared, high above the swamplands, using the thermals to glide. She'd learned how to do that from watching hawks. Cradled by warm winds, she drifted lazily.

She was a genetic freak, with the DNA of predator plants

in her veins. A freak who could fly like a bird. But she never thought of herself as a freak. She never thought of herself as Toni either. She thought of herself as a Venus Angel, Viridian's greatest creation.

'I may die,' he'd told her. 'But you are my legacy. You are the Future.'

Toni made great sweeps over the swampland, patrolling her territory, queen of all she surveyed, the most powerful predator by far.

Suddenly, she stopped, hanging in mid-air, hovering, the tiny ancillary wings on her wrists and ankles beating hummingbird fast.

She'd seen something.

Down there, among all the different shades of green something dark, glossy green was moving, sliding through the pitcher plants. Whatever it was, it had chlorophyll skin, like her.

She stared down, trying to make it out. Was it a Verdan who hadn't been given the vaccine yet? But Verdans never came here.

Suddenly, as she watched, it flashed red, like a warning signal.

Toni shook her head. 'No, no, no.'

Then it flashed again, two great blood-red ovals. And now Toni had to believe. There was another Venus Angel down there. And she knew, by the colour its wings were inside, that it had been stealing her food.

Viridian had told her she was unique, that she was the only one. But he'd lied.

Toni gave a great screech of rage.

Her eyes flashing fury, she came hurtling down out of the sky to defend her kingdom.

CHAPTER THREE

Jay was wandering around Franklin.

There was a big community thing going on. Townsfolk were working together, finding their families, moving back into their houses. People were giving out food supplies.

Even the shops were opening up again. Most of them had closed when the world went Verdan. Verdans hadn't wanted anything shops could sell them. They got all they needed from the natural world around them.

Maybe Dad could get a new trailer, thought Jay. Maybe he could open up Rainbirds Diner again, selling burgers to truckers on the motorway.

Jay was trying to pretend. But he knew things weren't anywhere near back to normal.

He kicked out at a stone. He was killing time. He was in a fever to get going to find Toni; he didn't want to wait until tomorrow. But he didn't dare push Dad any further. Jay didn't trust him not to change his mind about the whole thing.

If he does that, thought Jay, *he can go to hell. I'll go on my own.*

He thought about going round to Gran's. She'd brought him up, always been there, when Dad wasn't. But now Jay didn't totally trust her, either.

He thought of Gran when she'd turned Verdan, with her clammy green skin, her green candyfloss hair. She'd been like an alien, thought Jay, shuddering. He remembered her creepy green eyes, sliding away from her own grandson as if he wasn't important any more. How she'd said, 'Move out of my way, you're shading my light.'

She was human again now. When Dr Moran discovered the cure, she'd rushed to get it, like all the other Verdans.

But Jay could never forget that she'd tried to betray him to the Immune Hunters. She'd yelled, 'There's an Immune here. A dirty, selfish polluter! Come and arrest him!'

It wasn't her fault, Jay told himself. *They were all brainwashed by Viridian. They were terrified of his warriors.*

But he knew he could never trust Gran again, like he had before.

The only person he trusted was Toni. In a mad world, he clung to his memories of her like a shipwrecked traveller clings to a lifebelt.

She'd come with him to rescue Dad, that time he got caught by Viridian. She was the only one who'd helped him. He owed her.

Well, I'm going to help her *now*, Jay told himself. *I'm going to find her, give her the vaccine, bring her back home with me to Franklin.*

Then everything would be all right.

Lost in his dreams, Jay had wandered through the little town, to its scrubby edge lands, where straggly trees and bramble bushes choked the ground. Jay followed a track through them. Suddenly, he stopped dead.

He'd almost walked into a weird-looking tent. Its top was suspended from a tree and the bottom reached the ground. It was shaped like a teepee and made of white gauzy stuff.

'What's that?' wondered Jay aloud.

Inside the tent was a squirming mass – thousands of black wormy things, wriggling around, busy doing something.

Alarmed, Jay backed off. Then he realized what he was looking at. 'You're so jumpy,' he mocked himself, grinning.

Living through Viridian's evil reign had made him like that, always on the run, always looking over his shoulder for Immune Hunters.

'It's just caterpillars, you wuss,' he told himself.

He'd seen this before. Sometimes caterpillars spun tents over bushes and trees, covering them completely, as if they'd been draped with huge wedding veils. Then they munched up the leaves inside, undisturbed. When the tree was just bare skeleton twigs, they moved on.

Feeling bolder, Jay knelt down to peer through the silky gauze. A green arm ripped through the gauze and flopped right into his face.

Jay yelled out and fell backwards, his heart racing. He scrambled up, ready to run. But then he saw that the arm lay limp and unmoving. Its fingers were curled up, like a dead spider. Fingers, hand and arm were spotted with circles of black fungus.

Jay's panicky heartbeat began to slow down.

Still he waited and watched for a few minutes longer, just to be sure. Not one finger twitched. The arm was half-eaten anyway, its chlorophyll skin munched by caterpillars.

'It's a dead Verdan,' Jay decided. Probably one that hadn't got the vaccine in time and had been killed by the black spot fungus.

He knelt down again, to inspect the arm. Then he realized this was no ordinary Verdan. The arm had once been massive and muscular, like a bodybuilder's, with bulging veins snaking around it.

'Immune Hunter,' Jay spat out.

He kicked the arm viciously. *Good riddance*, he thought.

Then an amazing thought rocked him, like a starburst inside his head.

Maybe this wasn't an Immune Hunter either. Maybe it was the corpse of the mighty Viridian himself. Was this where the great tyrant had crawled to die? Was this how he'd ended up, with a million caterpillars feeding on his body?

Jay felt himself trembling; he just couldn't help it. 'You've got to check this out,' he told himself.

If it was Viridian, everyone would want to know about it. Everyone in Franklin kept telling each other, 'He's dead, for sure.' But there'd been no actual *proof*, so far.

Jay could see himself, bringing back the good news to the town, shouting it out in the streets. 'I've found him! The green freak is really dead!' And all the citizens of Franklin would go crazy, cheering and whooping with joy. The street parties would probably go on for days.

Jay knelt down. He picked up the long-dead arm. 'Urgh.' He almost dropped it when he saw caterpillars wriggle from the veins and scurry away.

He felt like throwing up. But he had to make sure. Fighting nausea, Jay inspected the arm carefully, turned it over.

At last, he let the arm go.

'It's not him,' he said, out loud. He let out a long, ragged breath. 'It's not Viridian.'

After the Verdan scientists developed grafting, Viridian had had a Venus fly trap implanted into his wrist. Not as a weapon, because it was too tiny; it could only kill insects. Maybe he'd wanted it as personal jewellery to decorate his glossy green skin. Or maybe so he could feed it with flies, like a pet.

But this arm had no tiny Venus fly trap. It had other implants, proper Immune-killing plant weapons, some spines on the palm that had once been deadly poisonous to humans. Jay almost touched them, but warned himself, *Don't. They could still be dangerous, like wasps can sting you after they're dead.*

Jay had spent months running from Immune Hunters, hiding out with Dad in the old mine tunnels under Franklin. It would be really stupid if a dead one finally killed him.

Slowly, wearily, Jay hauled himself to his feet.

For a moment, huge disappointment weighed him down. He would have liked to have found Viridian's body. It would have been great news to tell Toni, when he found her. He could imagine how thrilled she'd be, after all the monster had done to her, forcing her to become Verdan and have those terrible wings put on her back.

He left the dead Immune Hunter to the munching caterpillars and stumbled off through the wasteland.

But thinking of Toni raised Jay's spirits. *We'll be seeing each other*, he told himself. *Really soon*. He knew where he and Dad would look first. Dr Moran had told them about some swamplands, south of Franklin. It was the kind of place, he'd said, where a Venus Angel, with carnivorous plant DNA in her body, might feel at home.

Jay replayed the conversation in his head. He'd confronted Dr Moran and furiously asked, 'Why aren't we going to find Toni? I'm sick of waiting! Why do you keep putting it off?'

'Because I'm needed more here,' Dr Moran had answered. 'And besides, if Toni wants to be cured, she knows where we are. What's stopping her coming home?'

Jay had secretly asked himself that very same question. Every day, since Toni flew off, he'd scanned the skies, longing to see her flying back. But she never came.

Jay had given Dr Moran all the excuses he gave himself: 'Could be lots of things stopping her. Maybe she's in trouble. Maybe she needs our help. Maybe she's lost...'

'Or maybe,' Dr Moran had interrupted him, 'she's in the swamplands. And maybe she likes it there. Maybe she doesn't *want* to be found.'

Not by you she doesn't, you cold-hearted creep, Jay had thought, staring at Dr Moran with his eyes full of scorn.

Suddenly, Jay felt a stinging pain. A spiky bramble branch had raked his arm. He licked off the beads of blood and stared around. He was in a derelict industrial estate, abandoned long ago, even before the virus. Grass grew in the car parks and tree saplings and ivy burst through the broken windows.

I know this place, Jay thought, shuddering.

Under his feet was the old lead mine, with miles of tunnels and caves, where he and Dad had hidden.

Over there was an open trapdoor. It was the entrance to the Etiolation Cave, where Viridian had punished any Verdan who opposed him, or was suspected of being an Immune Sympathiser. He'd imprisoned them in darkness, until, like plants deprived of light, their green skin became sickly yellow and their limbs weak and floppy.

Gran had been shut up in here. Jay had rescued her in time. But he hadn't been able to save Teal, Viridian's rival for the top job of Cultivar Commander.

An image flashed into Jay's mind, of Teal in the Etiolation Cave, chained to a rock, her body being slowly rotted by fungus into yellow jelly. She'd died as he'd knelt helplessly by her side.

It was only later he'd found out that Teal was Toni's mother. But, for his own reasons, he had never told Toni about Teal's death. He'd let her carry on believing her mum was still alive.

He felt ashamed now when he thought about that.

I'll definitely tell her when I find her again, Jay promised himself.

He walked over to the open trapdoor. There was nothing to fear now that Viridian's reign was over. There were no Verdans down there suffering. There were no Verdans much anywhere. Soon, when every single one had been given the vaccine and developed antibodies to the plant virus, the Verdan species would be as extinct as the dinosaurs.

But still, Jay's heart was pounding. He peered down into the Etiolation Cave. He couldn't see much, apart from the top few steps of the stone stairway down. Beyond that, there was darkness.

He turned away. He was about to walk off when, suddenly, he felt a vice-like grip on his leg. Shocked and bewildered, he looked down. An arm had come out of the trapdoor entrance. Its bony fingers clutched his ankle. Another arm shot out, clasping his left ankle. It was like he'd been clamped in leg irons. Then, before Jay could even scream out in terror, he was dragged underground and the trapdoor slammed shut behind him.

CHAPTER FOUR

J ay was being hustled away from the Etiolation Cave through a maze of underground passages.

His two captors were human, not Verdan. But they looked like wild men, filthy and half-starved, with scraggy beards and dirty bare feet. Their clothes fluttered in tatters. Their hair was stiff with soil; soil was in every crease of their skin.

At first Jay fought back but their grip was incredibly strong. No matter how he twisted and kicked he couldn't escape. They held on relentlessly.

He cried out, 'Where are you taking me?'

But they didn't answer. And when he stared into their faces for some human response their eyes were empty, as if they were zombies, without minds of their own.

Then, through the grime and hair, he recognized one.

'Mr Jacobs?' he said. Mr Jacobs had been Jay's head teacher at Franklin High. He always used to wear smart grey suits, with a handkerchief in his top pocket that matched his tie. Jay remembered him, after he'd got the virus, making a stirring speech in the school hall. 'Everyone should be

Verdan! It's like being born again. We Verdans will heal our planet. We'll make the Earth a paradise once more, like it was before humans polluted it.'

'Mr Jacobs,' Jay begged him. 'You know me. It's Jay Rainbird. I was at your school. Tell me what's going on. What are you doing down here?'

But Mr Jacobs just gazed at his ex-pupil from blank, hollow eyes.

Jay was frogmarched through tunnels. It wasn't fully dark; more like a twilight world. Dim light filtered down from ventilation shafts, and luminous fungi sprouting from the tunnel floor cast an eerie glow over everything.

The fungi were star-shaped and gleamed ghostly white. Every time Jay trod on one, they puffed out fungus spores that drifted like smoke through the tunnels.

Strangely, his panic was draining away. He stopped struggling and asking frantically, 'Where are you taking me?' He just stumbled along, woozy and disconnected, all the time crushing those star-shaped fungi under his feet and breathing in their spores.

Jay's captors let go of his arms. He could have escaped. But it never even occurred to him. He just padded after them, like an obedient dog.

As if in a dream, he saw people digging. Slaving away, crouched in tunnels. He saw children, dirty and blank-eyed. Some were digging, struggling to lift heavy picks, like the child miners of two hundred years ago. Some were marching about like little machines, taking water to other zombie slaves, carrying soil away. Everyone was working away like robots. The clanging of spades and picks on rock echoed through the mine.

But Jay didn't ask himself, *What's going on here?* He didn't feel scared, or even worried. There was a fog spreading through his brain, and he couldn't feel much at all.

Those weird fungi were everywhere, crowding the tunnel floors. Some were dying, collapsing into black slime. But more were coming up all the time. Incuriously, Jay watched them, punching up from the soil like tiny white skulls, then breaking open into stars, making the air cloudy with their spores.

Jay was taken through a cave. Dreamily, he thought, *I've been here before.*

The cave had a jet floor that glittered like black glass. When they were hiding out, Jay and Dad had skated in here, sliding about on the jet, colliding and falling, laughing their heads off like two kids on a frozen pond in winter.

But the memory drifted out of Jay's mind. He forgot about Dad altogether and anything to do with his past. He even forgot his own name.

He found himself in another cave very close by. His captors had melted away but other humans shuffled in and stood in a submissive crowd, as if waiting for something. Like him, their clothes weren't filthy and ragged; their skin wasn't grimed with dirt. He stared blankly at them, unsurprised.

The cave soared around him as high as a cathedral. A garden of luminous fungi glowed on the walls: purple jelly blobs, orange fungi that flowed like slime, toadstools that gleamed sickly white. On the floor the ghostly stars were shining, as if they'd fallen from the heavens and were trapped down here, in this subterranean world. He looked at it all without interest.

The air was rich with the smell of mould and decay. The clouds of spores seemed thicker here, more concentrated. He breathed them in, without even noticing.

A chittering sound came from somewhere above him. He raised dull eyes, trying to see through the spore haze. High up in the cave roof bats were hanging, in a squeaking, rustling cluster. One flew out, swooped around and landed again.

Then he heard another sound. A voice was speaking. 'Welcome, Fungoids,' it said, 'to my Kingdom.'

Slowly, the new slave turned his head. Hardly anything was registering now in his drugged brain. But there was just enough of his old self left to whisper, 'Viridian?'

The creature he was staring at was nothing like the Viridian he had known before. At the height of his powers, as Verdan Supreme Commander, Viridian had been a magnificent monster, almost three metres tall, with green glossy skin and a Mohican crest of vicious thorns. He was just seventeen. But he'd been mesmeric, terrifying, his eyes burning with green fire, like a teenage warlord come from another galaxy to claim planet Earth as his kingdom.

Now he'd morphed into a completely different kind of monster: a hulk with pale eyes and waxy-white, rubbery limbs. But his voice hadn't changed. It boomed out with the same cruel swagger. His eyes still burned with the same fanatical self-belief.

Viridian was still alive. If his newest slave had had any hope left, it died at that moment.

Viridian gazed at this fresh batch of subjects snatched from the streets of Franklin. He knew they were completely in his power: zombie slaves with no minds of their own. Their function now was as diggers, to expand his underground empire far beyond Franklin, and to kidnap fresh slaves from the surface wherever they tunnelled. They would work themselves to death in his service. Or be crushed in rock falls, or drowned in flash floods. But to Viridian that was only right. Their dead bodies would still be useful to him. And, besides, there were plenty more humans up there to replace them.

Viridian had massive plans. The black spot fungus, instead of killing him, had mutated him into this new hybrid. He was much further away from human but a hundred times more powerful than he'd ever been as a Verdan.

His body gave off a sinister glow, like the toadstools on his cave wall. The skin across his skull was as slippery smooth as the cap of the deadly poisonous amanita mushroom, whose common name is Destroying Angel. Crowning his head, instead of Verdan thorns, was a great pleated crest, shaped like an axe blade. And from his luminous fingers spun strange, long, sticky threads that stretched away into darkness.

'Fungoids,' said Viridian, his voice low now and heavy with menace. 'You will obey me in everything. But, should you ever dream of rebelling, know this. I do not need to move from my cave. I am everywhere. I know everything. And I will live *forever*.'

Then, along with the rest of the zombie army, Viridian's newest Fungoid shuffled away into the dark tunnels.

CHAPTER FIVE

J ay opened his eyes and saw a dazzling light above him. He grimaced in pain.

A single thought somehow slipped through the fog in his brain. *My eyes hurt.* So he closed them, turned his head aside, and sank back into the soft bed he seemed to be lying on.

For many hours he slipped in and out of consciousness, not knowing where, or who he was. Each time he woke he felt like death.

Finally he woke up with the sun warming his body.

But, this time, he didn't close his eyes again. Instead, he started trying to make sense of things. It was slow work. His brain was still hazy and there was a sickening graveyard smell of mould and decay in his nostrils.

Jay saw a hand flopped open in front of him. He stared at it. It was blurry and out of focus. He blinked, and the hand became clear. It had black fingernails and was criss-crossed with cuts. There were big blisters on the palm.

Whose hand is that? thought Jay.

It was dead white. It looked like it belonged to a corpse. After a while he realised that it was his own. Experimentally, he made the finger wriggle. Some cuts split open and began to bleed.

I'm alive, thought Jay.

For a while he lay, flat on his back, watching the drifting clouds form themselves into castles and mountain ranges, then break up and make other shapes.

He'd last done this when he was a little boy on lazy, hot days in Gran's back garden.

Finally he told himself, *This is no good, Jay. You can't stay here forever.*

So he sat up, hugging his knees to stop them shaking. He gazed around. He'd been lying high up on a bank of soft grass and wild flowers. Below him, in the stream bed, a whole tree was wedged. It was smashed and splintered as if it had been left behind by a raging torrent. But there was no torrent there now, just a trickle of water, sliding between the rocks.

Cautiously, Jay checked himself over. His feet were bare and his toenails long and jagged. There were livid bruises, turning yellow, green and purple, all over his arms and legs. But, otherwise, his skin and ragged clothes had been washed clean.

You're all right, Jay. Stop messing about and stand up, he ordered himself.

He tried standing up.

'Whoa,' he said, as his head started spinning. He sat back down and lifted his face to the warm breeze. It seemed ages since he'd felt wind on his skin, fresh air in his lungs. He took several deep breaths and felt better.

Suddenly images, all mixed up, came slamming into his head. He was sweating in a dark cramped space, hands gripping a pick handle that was wet with his blood. He was struggling in black, swirling water, fighting for air.

He was in a jewelled cave, watching...

As this flashback hit him, Jay shot to his feet, his face a mask of horror.

He looked round frantically, trying to get his bearings. In the distance he could see the twin gothic towers of Franklin's town hall.

On wobbly legs, he began staggering in that direction. He wasn't thinking at all: he didn't dare. He just focussed on keeping his legs going, pumping air into his lungs. People he stumbled past in the Main Street of Franklin saw his wild eyes and haunted expression. But they didn't pay any attention. In the chaos after the virus, many citizens, still traumatized, unable to find their families, were wandering like lost souls around Franklin with the same tormented looks.

When Jay was almost at Franklin High, he saw Dad coming out of the building.

Dad stared, as if, at first, he hardly recognised his own son. Then relief and joy flooded his face.

'Jay!' he yelled. He came racing up and clasped Jay in a big bear hug. Then he stood back so he could get a good look at him. 'What on earth happened to you? Where have you been?'

Jay, swaying wearily, couldn't get the words out. They seemed to be trapped in his throat.

'I've been looking all over for you,' Dad rushed on. 'I thought you'd taken off on your own to find Toni. I thought – '

Dad broke off as words suddenly exploded from Jay's mouth: 'Viridian's not dead.'

For a few seconds, Dad gazed at Jay in shock and disbelief. Then he asked, 'What did you say, son?', as if he hoped his ears were playing tricks.

'He's alive, Dad,' Jay gasped. 'I saw him, with my own eyes. Viridian is still alive.'

CHAPTER SIX

'Let the poor kid eat something, get some rest,' said Dad. 'He looks like a wreck.'

'He can rest later,' said Dr Moran. 'After he's told us everything he remembers.'

They were in the basement of Franklin High where Dr Moran had his laboratories and Dad and Jay were living temporarily. Dr Moran had been grilling Jay for an hour, showing no mercy for his hunger and exhaustion.

But he was focussing on Jay with fierce attention as if every word he said was pure gold. Jay couldn't help liking the feeling of power that gave him.

Yeah, you're listening to me now, thought Jay, thinking about all the times Dr Moran had treated him some dumb kid who couldn't see the bigger picture, who put his own selfish needs, like wanting to rescue Dad or Toni, before Dr Moran's mission of saving the world.

'So we've established,' said Dr Moran, 'that Viridian is building an underground empire with this army of human slaves. That he's got some kind of power over their minds.

That you probably only escaped because a flash flood washed you out of the mine.'

'That green freak,' said Dad bitterly. 'I thought he was dead. What does he call himself now? Big Chief Fungoid or something? What's that mean? That he's some kind of monster mushroom, for God's sake?'

'It means,' said Dr Moran, grim-faced, 'that in this new mutation he could be more powerful than ever. Fungi are very ancient organisms, billions of years old. They ruled this planet before humans, dinosaurs, before plants even. They've got powers you wouldn't believe. They feed on death and decay. They're the ultimate recyclers. They can live forever.'

'Yeah,' said Jay, suddenly remembering. 'Viridian said, "I am Immortal".'

Dad muttered, 'You're kidding me.' But Jay could see him rubbing at the tattoos on his wiry arms, as if he was slowly realizing that the Viridian nightmare might be starting again.

'What else did he say?' Dr Moran asked urgently. 'Can you remember?'

Jay frowned. It was hard to work out what had happened to him down in the mine. Most of it was still a blank. But, in bits and pieces, some of it was coming back to him.

'He said,' Jay told Dr Moran, scowling with the effort of remembering, '"I do not need to move from my cave. I am everywhere. I know everything."'

Jay pictured Viridian's great, brutal head swinging round, like a crested dinosaur. He saw those alien eyes gazing at him, pale and spooky, from a place no human could reach.

Had Viridian recognised him? Jay told himself, *No*, even though they'd once been blood brothers, mixing Jay's red human blood with the green sap that bled from Viridian's veins.

'What would Viridian bleed now?' said Jay, hardly realising he was speaking out loud.

'Lactose,' guessed Dr Moran. 'It's a milky fluid most fungi have inside them.'

Jay shivered. 'What kind of a ghoul is he?'

'Look, we have to focus,' said Dr Moran. 'We know what he's doing but not how. Just where was this cave?'

'I can't exactly remember. I know it was near the cave where me and Dad skated…'

'Skated?' said Dr Moran, baffled.

Dad chipped in to explain. 'This other cave he's talking about, it's got a polished jet floor. Don't know who did that – maybe the old lead miners.'

'OK,' said Dr Moran, patiently. 'So we have some vague idea where Viridian's cave is. Now tell me what he looked like.'

'I already told you once,' Jay protested. 'He had this weird thing on his head.'

'Yes, yes.' Dr Moran shrugged, as if it wasn't what he wanted to hear. 'Pleated, like the gills under a mushroom cap. That's probably not functional, it just makes him look extra menacing. But was there anything else? Any other features of fungi?'

'How'd you expect him to know?' objected Dad. 'The only thing he knows about mushrooms is that they come sliced on top of pizzas.'

But Jay had recalled something else. 'Viridian had this sticky string-stuff like, I don't know, white candyfloss or something, coming out of his hands. Like long, long strings. Is that important?'

'Yes,' said Dr Moran, his cold eyes sparking, as if, at last, he was on to something. 'Where did these strings go?'

'I'm not sure,' said Jay, struggling to remember. 'Seemed like, into the ground?'

'Then they're hyphae,' said Dr Moran, shaking his head in stunned disbelief. 'What else could they be?'

'You asking me?' said Jay. 'Look, I'm shattered, my hands hurt, can we do this tomorrow?'

But Dr Moran didn't seem to hear. 'He's using the power of fungi for world domination,' he was saying, in an awed whisper. 'It's incredible. Biologically, it's brilliant.'

'We're not all plant scientists,' said Dad. 'What the hell are you talking about?'

Dr Moran fired another question at Jay. 'Were there other fungi in the tunnels, apart from in Viridian's cave?'

'All over the place,' said Jay. 'Lots of them were shaped like stars.'

38

'Earthstars,' said Dr Moran. He grabbed a book from a pile stacked in the basement corner. He flicked through and showed Jay a photo.

'Yeah, that's them,' Jay agreed.

'You know how they got there?' said Dr Moran, more excited than Jay had ever seen him. 'Viridian's growing them, from his own body. Those sticky threads you spoke about, they're called hyphae. Viridian sends them out, they can grow for miles underground. Every so often, they branch upwards and grow an earthstar on the surface. And I bet those earthstars puff out spores, tiny seeds, like clouds of dust. Am I right?'

'How'd you know that?' said Jay.

'Because that's what fungi do,' said Dr Moran. 'These clouds of spores, did you breathe them in?'

'Couldn't help it,' said Jay, remembering how the spores had made him cough at first.

'Why are these spore things important?' said Dad. 'You've lost me.'

'Don't you see?' said Dr Moran. 'These zombie slaves Jay spoke about. It's how Viridian controls their minds. He can reach them wherever they're digging, even miles away, just by sending out hyphae to grow earthstars that puff out more spores. The slaves are breathing them in all the time.'

'So?' Dad shrugged. 'I still don't get it.'

But Jay did. He remembered how, the more he breathed them in, the woozier he became, how his wits slipped away from him. 'Those spores affect your brain, don't they? Make you like a zombie, so you do whatever Viridian wants.'

Dr Moran nodded in approval. 'Exactly right,' he said. 'As I said, he's using the power of fungi. There's a fungus in Indonesia – when ants breathe in its spores, their behaviour changes. They become like zombies. It's here somewhere.'

He flicked through the book, stopped on a page for a moment, then said quickly, 'This photo's not very good.' He covered it with his hand. 'Anyway, these spores give off chemicals that affect the ants' brains. Only Viridian's doing it with people. Fascinating.'

'You almost sound like you admire the creep,' said Dad.

'What happens to the ants?' Jay said. 'The ones that breathe in the spores?'

Doctor Moran hesitated, as if he was deciding what to say.

'What happens?' Jay asked again.

Some instinct made him snatch the book off Dr Moran. Before the doctor could protest, Jay had seen the photo. It was of an ant, with what looked like cotton wool growing out of its body, sprouting from the top of its head.

'What's the white stuff?' said Jay.

'A kind of fungus,' Dr Moran told him. 'The spores don't just release chemicals. They actually grow into fungus inside the ants. The fungus spreads through their bodies...'

'Then what happens?' Jay interrupted. 'Tell me.'

'They die, eventually,' Dr Moran admitted. 'Although it may take some time.'

'Is that going to happen to me?' Jay whispered, staring, mesmerized at the photo. 'I breathed in the spores. Is a fungus growing inside *me*?'

'Tell him it's not,' Dad commanded Dr Moran. 'Just because it happens to ants doesn't mean it will happen to him, does it?'

Dr Moran took a deep breath. 'That's true,' he agreed. 'And Jay didn't breathe them for long. It seems as though, when you stop breathing them in, you get back to normal quite quickly. It seems that there are no ill effects.'

'See?' said Dad. 'You're going to be all right, son. Isn't he, doc?

'Yes,' said Dr Moran. 'It seems there's no need to worry.'

But, unlike Dad, Jay had noticed how Dr Moran had been careful to say, three times, 'it seems.'

He stared at Dr Moran's troubled face and thought, *You don't know for sure, do you? You don't know those spores aren't growing inside me. You're just pretending you do so I don't freak out.*

Jay stood up, 'I'm going to get a shower,' he said. 'Chuck these clothes away.'

Emotions were crashing over him in waves. His suspicion that, despite what Dr Moran said, fungus might be growing inside him, was the last straw. He just couldn't cope any more. He didn't know whether to get violent and punch somebody, or break down and cry like a baby. Instead he burst out, wildly, 'So what about Toni? No one's even mentioned her name! Have you forgotten about her?' He whirled round to face Dad. 'How long have I been missing?'

'Two weeks,' said Dad. 'And two days.'

'That's nearly six weeks since she flew away. *Anything* could have happened to her.'

'Stop thinking about that green freak,' said Dad. 'She isn't thinking about you, that's for sure. She's forgotten you, Jay, just face it. That's what Verdans do, forget their friends and family. If she hasn't, why isn't she back here?'

'Shut up!' screamed Jay. 'Why don't you just shut up? You always spoil everything!'

Only Dr Moran's stern command, 'Sit down!', stopped Jay from going for Dad's throat.

'Look,' said Dr Moran, his brisk, chilly tones cutting through the red mist in Jay's brain. 'We've got enough problems without fighting amongst ourselves. We have to find a way to stop Viridian. He can make humans slaves. He can extend his empire underground. He's a bigger threat than the plant virus.'

'He can't tunnel under oceans though, can he?' Dad argued. 'He can't spread his empire world-wide, like he tried to do before?'

'I'm not so sure about that,' said Dr Moran.

'What about Toni?' pleaded Jay, feeling weak and helpless after his fit of rage.

But Dr Moran wasn't listening to him any more. Clutching the book about fungi, he marched off.

He was just going into his lab when a thought seemed to strike him. 'Don't throw your clothes away,' he told Jay. 'Leave them outside the bathroom door.'

'Why?' demanded Jay. 'They're just rags.'

'Because there may be earthstar spores in them,' said Dr Moran.

'I was in a flash flood,' Jay protested, remembering how he was washed up on the bank, soggy, half drowned, coughing up river water. 'The spores can't be still there.'

'Some may be,' said Dr Moran. 'Perhaps trapped in the seams. I want to examine them under a microscope, see how they work.'

He disappeared into his lab. Jay stared after him with hate-filled eyes.

'I didn't expect him to care,' Jay told Dad. 'But you said *you'd* come.' His voice was sounding aggressive again.

'Look, cool down,' said Dad. 'Get control of yourself. Or I'm leaving.'

'What, you mean, getting on your bike?' Jay spat out. 'Going off again, abandoning me?'

'No, you idiot,' said Dad. 'I mean, leaving the room.'

There was silence, as Jay's mind went hurtling again down a rollercoaster of bitter emotions.

Then, suddenly, to his total surprise, he found himself with a shaky smile on his face.

'Think you're funny, don't you?' Jay said, and he and Dad grinned at each other.

He took a few deep breaths. 'OK, I'm cool. It's just Dr Moran, he winds me up. But you did say you'd come with me. We were all ready to go when I got snatched.'

Dad looked uneasy. 'Don't get mad again,' he said. 'But things have changed now, after what you told us about Viridian. We have to protect ourselves. We need to find all the ways down to that mine. Any place where those Fungoid freaks could snatch people. We need to block those holes up. If they dig new ones we need to block those too. You know I'm right.'

Jay sighed and shrugged. 'Yeah, you're right.'

'From what you said,' added Dad, 'those slaves are digging longer and longer tunnels. I mean, they could be right under our feet.'

Jay had to admit that Dad had changed. From being Mr Unreliable, who Gran said had never grown up, he'd become the leader of Franklin's survivors, the guy people looked to for practical help. Unlike Dr Moran, shut away in his lab, Dad rolled up his sleeves and got stuck in.

But that's no use to me and Toni, Jay thought. He felt as alone as he had done when he was small, when Dad was always away somewhere, touring the world on his motorbike.

Jay headed for the door.

'Where are you going?' asked Dad.

'For a shower, like I said,' Jay told him. But there was a steely determination in Jay's mind. He was sick of waiting for Dad and Dr Moran. He knew, if he wanted to find Toni, he could only depend on himself. And if the fungus was growing inside him, how long did he have? He'd wasted enough time already.

Dad said, 'Before you have that shower, come and see my new truck.'

'What new truck?' said Jay. 'I'm in a hurry.'

'Come and see,' Dad coaxed him.

He led Jay upstairs. Parked outside, on what had once been Franklin's High's football pitch, was an old farm truck that looked like it had been carrying sheep and hay bales around for ever. It had a row of mangled teddy bears, some missing eyes and limbs, lashed to the bull bars in front, like some kind of sick joke.

'You do that?' said Jay, jerking his thumb towards the bull bars.

'What, the teddy bears? They were there when I got it. I never got round to cutting them off.'

'Where'd you get the truck?' asked Jay.

'I picked it up off the street,' Dad shrugged. 'Why not? Those Verdans just left all their cars to rust.'

'It's not new,' said Jay, already turning away, his mind on other things.

'I know,' said Dad. 'But she's an old workhorse. She can tackle any terrain. She's what we'll go to find Toni in.'

'Yeah?' said Jay. Suddenly Dad had got all his attention. In rising excitement, he said, 'You really mean it, Dad? When can we start?'

'Well,' said Dad, 'I need to get some fuel first. That might take a while.'

Jay's hopes were dashed to the ground again. 'I thought you meant we were going, like, now. What did you show me your crummy old truck for? It can't even go anywhere. It's useless.' Jay aimed a kick at a truck tyre.

'Look, be reasonable, Jay,' Dad pleaded. 'We will go, I promise. But we need to wait until it calms down out there. There are Immune Hunters in the woods. There are vigilantes after them. Some vigilantes swore they'd seen a couple of Venus Angels, in the sky, far away. That's weird,' added Dad. 'I thought Toni was the only one.'

'Where?' demanded Jay, his voice shifting in a second from angry to urgent. '*Where* did they see Venus Angels?'

'Somewhere over the swamplands,' said Dad. 'Where Dr Moran said she'd be.'

'These vigilantes,' said Jay, feeling his heart racing, his blood roaring in his ears. 'Do they think Toni was an Immune Hunter?'

'Who knows what those guys think?' said Dad. 'They're trigger-happy. They're firing at everything with green skin. Wait, son!'

But Jay was already gone, back inside, down to the basement.

He didn't head to the shower first, but to Dr Moran's laboratory. He wanted to steal some of the tiny dropper bottles filled with the vaccine that cured the plant virus.

46

He thought Dr Moran would try to stop him, that he'd guess Jay wanted it for Toni.

But Dr Moran wasn't thinking about Toni. He was thinking about Viridian's new Fungoid transformation. 'His hyphae must have two purposes,' mused Dr Moran, as soon as he saw Jay. 'They grow earthstars but they also carry nutrients back to Viridian. That's how he stays alive.'

The last thing Jay wanted was a biology lecture. But he wanted to keep Dr Moran sweet, so he could steal the bottles. So he said, 'What nutrients?'

'From dead organisms,' answered Dr Moran. Now he had his head buried in his book, so he didn't see Jay sneaking closer to the vaccine cupboard. 'The hyphae rot them down, absorb their nutrients. I told you, fungi can do that.'

Jay put two bottles in his pockets. He froze as Dr Moran looked up from the pages as if he'd suddenly solved a problem. 'Does he use his slaves for food? Their dead bodies? That would be the most sensible way to feed himself. It's a really efficient system. No waste at all.'

A scene started replaying inside Jay's brain. He didn't want it to, but he couldn't stop it. He was back down the mine, stumbling on earthstars, breathing in their spores. And he'd almost tripped over something. It was a sticky mass of threads, like a fuzzy white blanket, growing on something huddled beneath.

Jay shuddered. Had it been a dead slave? Being rotted down to provide food for Viridian?

'You remember, don't you?' said Dr Moran, fixing Jay with his piercing gaze.

Jay shook his head, savagely, to drive out the terrible images. He didn't want to think any more about Viridian, his human slaves, or his hellish, decaying empire underground. His mind was up in a cloudless blue sky with a Venus Angel.

Even stumbling back from Viridian's mines, he'd searched the heavens, in case Toni was flying home. But something must be keeping her away. So he had to find her, before those trigger-happy vigilantes did.

Leave me alone! Jay yelled, inside his head, at Dr Moran. *Just get off my back.* All the time his fingers were clenched round the two precious vaccine bottles hidden inside his pocket.

But what he said out loud was, 'No, I don't remember. I don't remember most of it.'

Dr Moran nodded, as if he understood that. 'Leave your clothes outside the bathroom,' he reminded Jay, before he went back to his book.

Somehow, with a superhuman effort, Jay stopped himself from setting out immediately to find Toni. He knew he was good for nothing in his present state. He took a long, hot soak in the shower to ease his bruised body. He dumped his clothes outside, as Dr Moran had asked. He made himself eat even though he was too tired to be hungry. Then he slept.

Next morning, he woke up, surprised that he hadn't had bad dreams. Or, if he had, he didn't remember.

The first thing he did was raid the kitchen. It was early; no-one else was about. Jay could hear Dad snoring as he tiptoed past his bedroom.

Good, thought Jay, stuffing food supplies in his backpack: some cans from before the virus, some bread and apples. He didn't want any more confrontations. He didn't want to get worked up again and lose his temper. He just wanted to get on the road and away from here.

The next thing he needed was more vaccine. So he headed for Dr Moran's laboratory. He planned on taking maybe ten more bottles.

Best to have more than you need, Jay told himself. What if some bottles got lost somehow, or spilled or stolen?

He thought it would be simple, that he'd be in and out of the lab in seconds. But just as he was about to push open the door, he saw Dr Moran though the glass panel. Jay swore and ducked down.

Doesn't that guy ever sleep? he thought furiously.

Cautiously, he peered again into the lab.

Dr Moran was stooped over a microscope. He looked grey and haggard, as if he'd been up all night. Beside him on the bench, was Jay's T-shirt or what was left of it.

Jay guessed what Dr Moran was looking at.

He found spores, he told himself, *from one of Viridian's earthstars.*

Maybe Dr Moran could work out some scientific way of stopping Viridian, just as he'd found a way to cure the plant virus. But Jay knew that could take weeks, months. And, anyway, Viridian was Dr Moran's problem. Jay had other things on his mind.

He ducked down again and considered. Dr Moran was right in front of the vaccine cupboard. There was no way that Jay could steal some without him seeing.

You could wait until he comes out, thought Jay. Even Dr Moran must need a toilet break sometime.

But Jay knew he couldn't wait, couldn't risk Dad waking up. By that time, he wanted to be miles from here.

So he left.

You've got two bottles of vaccine, he reassured himself. *And it only takes one to cure Toni*. He'd just have to be extra careful with them, that was all.

He let himself out of the Franklin High basement, into a blazing red sunrise. He walked through the sleeping town and took the road south.

Jay had the whole motorway to himself. Verdans hadn't needed cars. And even though almost everyone was human again, there was still hardly any traffic. Most cars had rusted away and fuel was precious as gold dust. It was strictly rationed, for delivery lorries and emergency vehicles only. Besides that, the roads badly needed repairing. Grass was growing through the cracked tarmac and big potholes had opened up.

Don't go near them, Jay warned himself. You never knew which holes led to Viridian's underground kingdom. Or whether his zombie slaves would reach out and drag you down.

The fiery dawn had faded away. Now the sky curved above him, blue and cloudless. Yellow birds flickered through the hedges. A deer, grazing on the motorway, stared at him for a few seconds. Then it strolled away.

Jay took off his backpack and checked on the two tiny plastic bottles of vaccine inside.

It's OK, Jay reassured himself. *They're safe.*

And suddenly, walking in the sunshine down the empty motorway, Jay was surprised to find he was smiling.

For a while, he forgot about the terrors that weighed him down: Toni, vigilantes, the fungus that might be growing inside him. Instead, he felt light-headed with hope and the freedom of the wide open road.

It was two days' walk. There was a huge sprawling forest ahead, miles and miles of dark pines. You could get lost in there. But Jay had been to the forest before on an orienteering trip with his geography class. It seemed like ages ago in more innocent times. He still remembered the maps.

If you keep to the river, you can't get lost, he told himself.

And on the other side of the forest were the swamplands, which was where he'd find Toni.

He thought, *Bet she's waiting for me to get there.*

Even though all Verdans abandoned those they loved, even though his own gran had tried to betray him to the

Immune Hunters, Jay was convinced that Toni wasn't like other Verdans. That she still had feelings for him, hidden deep inside her plant hybrid body.

He took a can of beans out of his backpack. It didn't have a ring pull, so he sawed off the lid with a folding knife he'd taken from Dr Moran's lab. As he walked, he tipped the cold beans into his mouth for breakfast.

An hour later, he passed into the forest's cool shade.

In his lab, Dr Moran was still stooped over his microscope. He'd recovered a single spore from Jay's clothing.

'Amazing,' he murmured, as he sharpened the focus. 'I've never seen anything like this.'

Dr Moran rubbed his bleary eyes. He was so tired he could hardly see.

'Go outside,' he ordered himself. 'Take a walk around. Wake up.'

He let himself out of the basement, into the jungly wilderness that had once been a sports field. He took deep breaths of fresh air. But his brain was still busy thinking about Viridian, wondering about the extent of his powers, trying to work out how on earth humans could fight back. So Dr Moran didn't see the soil heaving and a hole appearing in the ground beside him. He didn't notice an arm sneaking out and its fingers, like a white tarantula, creeping nearer and nearer to his feet.

CHAPTER SEVEN

Two weeks before, when he'd seen her come screaming out of the sky, Thorn had been as surprised as Toni to find another Venus Angel.

Thorn had once been a boy called Mac. He'd been Jay's friend at Franklin High. But then he turned Verdan. He'd had a starry rise through the ranks. He'd quickly joined the Cultivars, top Verdans who got special privileges. But other Cultivars, jealous of Thorn's success, had set him up, told Viridian he was a traitor. Thorn was given two choices: death by etiolation, or to let Verdan scientists experiment on him in their search for the perfect warrior. Thorn had been taken, in chains, to a city in the north for the grafting surgery. When Viridian's regime fell, he'd escaped from the laboratories. And like Toni, when other Verdans rushed to be cured, Thorn had chosen to stay a Venus Angel.

That first time he'd seen Toni, hurtling down like an avenging fury, Thorn had flown away, searching for his own territory. But he'd found nowhere as good as the swamplands. So now he was back, to claim it as his own.

Toni was perched in a tree, her great wings clamped shut. She'd just finished digesting a crow. In a blaze of crimson and green, she shook out her wings and what was left of the crow, its bones, beak and a few black feathers, fell to the ground. With her long fingernails, she preened her wings, separating the spines that ran round the edges, so they'd be ready for her next prey.

Her green eyelids slid downwards. She seemed to be sleeping after her meal. But there was a part of her brain that was always alert, checking her territory for intruders.

She heard magpies chattering their alarm calls.

Her eyes shot open and her neck snaked around, this way, that, looking for danger. She scanned her swamps: the miles of tall ghostly pitcher plants, the bright green moss cushions that looked safe to land on but that concealed deep black bogs underneath.

Then she heard a swooshing above her, like the sound made by swans' wings, when they flew low over the swamplands,

Her fierce green eyes slid upwards. *There.*

Great wings beat above her, blocked out the sun. It was Thorn, trying to take her by surprise.

Enemy registered immediately in Toni's mind. She felt no fear at all; she was top predator. Her brain shrieked, *Attack!* Every nerve in her body tensed for the coming fight.

She exploded out of the tree. She knew she had to get higher than him. She soared upwards, as ever, seeking the sun.

She gave a scream of rage. Her wings beat uselessly above her as she tried to rise. Something was stopping her. She twisted round to look. Her right foot was trapped in her enemy's main wings, as he hovered below her, using his ankle and wrist wings to keep airborne.

His face was turned upwards to watch her struggles, his lips curving in a victor's smile.

'I am Thorn,' he shouted. 'And these swamplands are mine.'

Toni beat her wings harder, trying to drag him behind her. But, instead, he was dragging her down.

'No!' cried Toni.

In flight she was spectacular, aerobatic. But she feared being on the ground. There she was weak, like any puny human.

She tried to tug her foot free. But it was stuck fast. She could feel Thorn's wing spines piercing her ankle. Already, his digestive juices were burning her flesh.

Instead of trying to escape, she attacked. Her body was supple and whippy as a plant creeper. She looped it round until she was staring, upside down, right into Thorn's face. For a second, she hesitated, with the shock of seeing another Venus Angel so close. His alien green eyes were a mirror image of hers.

Then her predator's instincts took over. With wild, savage cries, she went for his eyes, stabbing with her long nails that she kept sharp for an extra weapon.

Thorn roared out in pain and anger. His main wings opened, just a fraction. But it was enough for Toni to yank her foot free. She soared up out of his reach and he followed, pursuing her in great sweeping circles across the sky. They climbed higher, their wings glittering in the sun.

Toni curled around in mid-air. Her wings were still beating strongly. But her foot burned like fire and her ankle was leaking green sap where Thorn's spines had stabbed it.

She bit her lip furiously, trying to ignore her wounds. She was a Venus Angel, Viridian's perfect Verdan. But she still felt pain like a human.

I've lost him, she thought, scanning the skies, empty except for a honking skein of geese in the distance. But then, like a green comet, Thorn came blazing in from the north, flying low, skimming the tops of the forest trees.

She thought, *I bet he learned from hawks*. His flying skills were good, maybe better than hers.

They clashed again right over the swamplands, smashing each other with great wing blows, screaming like sea eagles, trying to knock each other out of the sky.

Toni was tiring. She broke free and felt herself falling. Thorn was above her, he had the advantage. Desperately, she flapped her wings, climbing again. She knew it would be a fight to the death.

A crack echoed over the swamplands. Toni heard Thorn gasp above her. Then he went hurtling past her, spiralling downwards, his wings outspread.

Bewildered she watched him fall to earth. What was happening? She hadn't injured him that badly: a few rakes in his green flesh, a small tear in his wing, that was all.

Thorn vanished among the tall pitcher plants. Toni went swooping down after him.

The human vigilante, hidden in the pine trees that surrounded the swamplands, lowered his rifle.

Least I got one of them green freaks, he thought.

The other vigilantes would be jealous. Last week, in these woods, one had bagged a Green Vampire. They were big, dangerous brutes. They'd attack if they saw you first. But bringing down a Venus Angel was special. They were much rarer and harder to find.

Except, he hadn't got a trophy, like a piece of main wing, or maybe a small ancillary pair, to prove what he'd done. There was no way he was going to enter the treacherous swamplands. A man could sink in those bogs and drown, slowly. You could shout for help until you were hoarse but there'd be no-one around to hear you.

He shouldered his rifle and started to tramp off through the trees.

He'd just have to hope that the other vigilantes believed him when he boasted, 'I killed a Venus Angel.'

CHAPTER EIGHT

Jay was having terrible dreams. He dreamed that Toni had opened her Venus fly trap wings. He saw a human skull come tumbling out, the remains of her last meal, followed by a jumble of bones.

That's me, Jay thought. *That's my skeleton.* Somehow he was absolutely sure about that.

Then his dream shifted to another horror. He saw the photo of the dead ant, with fungus sprouting out of its brain. But the ant's body suddenly had a human head. And the human head had Jay's face on it.

Jay woke up, in the forest ferns where he'd crawled to sleep after his first day's walking. He was cold and shivering, drenched with dew. He lay there for a moment, his eyes closed, trying to shake off those two nightmare images.

The first one was easy to sneer at. 'Don't be stupid,' he muttered to himself. 'Toni couldn't eat people. They're too big. Anyway, she wouldn't eat *me*.'

But the second couldn't be laughed away. Yesterday, he'd kept up his spirits, striding out, happy and hopeful. Every time he thought of the earthstar spores, growing fungus inside his body, he'd told himself, *You're not going to die. Dr Moran said it wouldn't happen.*

Now, in the chilly dawn, his flesh crawling, he remembered the doubt in Dr Moran's eyes. And he was doubly sure that Dr Moran had been lying to him.

Jay had had everything all mapped out. When he found Toni and gave her the vaccine, they would be happy ever after.

But now he mocked himself mercilessly. 'Don't kid yourself. You and Toni might not be together long.'

It depended on Viridian's fungus, how long it took to spread and kill him. Would it be days? Or weeks?

Tears sprang to Jay's eyes; he couldn't help it. He was suddenly swamped by pity for himself and for Toni, having to face the future without him, all alone.

Then he heard a snuffling sound, very close.

Slowly, he became aware that something was sniffing his face. He smelled hot, rancid breath...

Jay's eyes shot open.

Dogs! his brain screamed at him. The Verdans had abandoned their pet dogs, because animals polluted the planet. The big dogs had eaten the little ones first, then they had gone feral and formed packs that hunted down deer and humans.

Jay tried to lie still. But he was trembling with fear. The nerves in his face twitched as the dog sniffed his ear.

59

The dog was a huge, wolf-like Alsatian with hungry eyes. Spiky twigs were tangled in its shaggy black and brown fur. It stopped sniffing. It had decided he wasn't Verdan. It hated the smell and taste of chlorophyll skin. It craved fresh meat and red blood.

It had still had a blue collar around its neck. A metal dog tag dangled from it. There was probably a name on that tag, the one humans had given it when it was a cute puppy. But the dog had forgotten that name.

The dog growled. It had him trapped now, straddling his body. Jay didn't dare move to get the folding knife out of his pocket.

He could hear the ferns shaking around him. Maybe other pack members were moving in, wanting their share.

Saliva dripped from the dog's jaw onto Jay's face. It was deciding where to bite him first.

Suddenly, another muzzle poked from the ferns. The Alsatian was distracted for a second. The hair along its spine bristled. It turned round to snap, savagely, at the smaller dog.

Jay grabbed his chance. He took off, scuttling on all fours through the ferns. And then the ferns ended and there was no more cover, so he shot to his feet and sprinted for the trees.

Adrenalin flooded through him and a sort of wild, reckless courage. The kind of courage you feel when there's nothing to lose. It took him completely by surprise.

You can make it, he found himself thinking.

A barking fury came streaking out of the ferns behind him. It was the Alsatian, hunting him down.

Jay, still running, checked over his shoulder and knew he couldn't outrun it. But his brain told him, *Stand and fight*. He grabbed a fallen tree branch then swung round to face the dog. As it attacked, he whirled around, striking out blindly with the branch, screaming out a savage war cry that hardly seemed to come from his own mouth.

Swaying with dizziness, dripping sweat, he had to stop after a few minutes. The Alsatian was still there. But it had backed off, snarling, watching to see what he would do next. Jay retreated too, a few paces, so his back was against a tree.

The Alsatian watched, its tongue lolling out, its eyes bright, expcctant, as if it knew he was already dog meat. It was just a mattcr of waiting.

Panting heavily, Jay grasped the branch, got ready for its next rush.

But then the other dog appeared again, a scrawny, yipping terrier. And it was all over in seconds. As the terrier approached too close, the Alsatian whisked round, grabbed it by the back of the neck and shook it once. The smaller dog didn't even have time to yelp. With the limp body dangling from its jaws, the Alsatian loped off into the ferns.

It didn't need Jay any more. It had its dinner now.

For a second Jay stared after it, paralysed with shock at that casual kill.

Then slowly, he slid down the tree trunk and slumped on the ground. The branch fell from his hand.

But that cool-thinking brain was still giving him orders. *You've got to get moving. The Alsatian might come back.*

First, he checked the two vaccine bottles weren't damaged. Then he forced himself shakily to his feet and headed south.

He thought again about the fungus growing towards his brain. But, this time, he didn't feel black despair. A new fighting spirit was burning inside him; a desperate, against-all-the-odds defiance. If he was already under a death sentence, why should any dangers on this journey scare him? He'd fought off that dog attack, hadn't he?

'You can go to hell, Viridian!' screamed Jay, as he crushed all thoughts of the fungus into a little box, padlocked the lid, and threw it down a deep, dark well in his mind. He pictured it, hurtling into blackness. Gone.

Then he stared around, as if he was seeing the forest for the first time.

For the first time in ages, his brain felt free from doubt and fear. His purpose seemed clear.

Find Toni, Jay commanded himself. *Just focus on that, and forget what comes after.*

He needed a better weapon. The folding knife was no good. So Jay picked up another branch from the forest floor. Suddenly, to his right, he saw the ferns ripple. Something was moving in there. The ripple was coming his way, like a green wave.

'Try your luck, you loser,' Jay murmured, grasping the branch in two hands like a baseball bat. 'You ain't gonna win.'

A Verdan woman slid out of the undergrowth, a stranger. 'Don't hurt me,' she begged.

Jay lowered the branch. She wasn't an Immune Hunter, just an ordinary Verdan, the kind Viridian had terrorized. And she looked sick. Her skin, which should have been green and glossy, was yellow. Plant diseases infested her body. There were circles of orange rust mould on her legs. Tiny red spider mites ran through her hair and clung onto her eyebrows and eyelashes. A slug was clamped to her neck. It had left a silvery trail where it had slithered along her skin.

'I need the vaccine,' she moaned.

Jay thought about the bottles of vaccine in his backpack.

'Why aren't you cured already?' he asked her. There was a mass, country-wide vaccination programme to eradicate the virus. She was the first ordinary Verdan he'd seen for weeks.

'I was hiding,' said the Verdan, looking fearfully around. 'I was hiding from those Green Vampires. They feed on us.'

'What?' said Jay. 'Who?'

The woman flicked the slug off her neck into the ferns. 'Don't you know about Green Vampires?'

'They some kind of Immune Hunter?' Jay guessed.

The Verdan nodded and shivered. 'They were only supposed to hunt down humans,' she told him. 'But they've turned on us now. They suck our plant sap, to top up their

63

own. It's how they stay strong. But they won't feed on me, not now I'm so sick. They only want healthy Verdans.'

'So do they still go after humans?' asked Jay.

'Yes,' said the woman. 'They still hate humans. They still kill them if they get the chance. But human blood's no use to them. It's plant sap they crave.'

The Verdan looked round at the dark trees, shuddering. 'When I'm human again,' she said, 'I won't ever come in here. I won't go to the river. They hide in the river.' Then she asked Jay, 'Tell me where I can be cured.'

Jay thought again about his two bottles of vaccine. He hardened his heart. *I can't help her*, he decided. He didn't dare give his spare bottle of vaccine to this stranger, even though she needed it so desperately. What if something happened to his last bottle and he had no vaccine for Toni?

'Walk north,' he told the Verdan woman, pointing out the way. 'Until you come to Franklin. They've got loads of vaccine there.'

The woman nodded. She didn't thank him. Her eyes slid indifferently away, as if she'd already dismissed him from her life.

He watched her walking off, seeking the splashes of light between the trees. Verdans loved the sunshine.

She'll make it, thought Jay. The wild dogs didn't eat Verdans and she'd said herself that she was too sick for these Green Vampires things to feed on. They wouldn't want to catch her diseases.

64

Yeah, she'll make it, Jay assured himself, confidently. The next time he saw her, she'd probably be human again.

He waved his stick in a last salute. 'Good luck,' he called to her. But she'd already slunk into the greenery.

Jay was suddenly struck by something the woman had said: 'They hide in the river.' He'd forgotten that Verdans could breathe underwater. They could generate their own oxygen from their chlorophyll skin.

Jay remembered how, before she'd turned Verdan, an Immune Hunter hiding deep in a pond had almost got Toni. He'd come blasting to the surface, a hulking green monster, his skin sparkling with oxygen bubbles. That one hadn't been a Green Vampire, whatever that might look like. He'd had other plant weapons. His hands sprouted hundreds of long sticky hairs, grafted from a jungle plant with glue strong enough to catch rats. He had grabbed Toni's hair with his sticky hands and Jay had had to hack off her long, brown tresses to free her.

Even that memory didn't give Jay the shivers. Nothing much scared him now. Except that thing in the locked box he'd thrown down the well.

He could see the river, glinting through the trees. If he followed it upstream, that would lead him straight to the swamplands.

As he walked with a light tread towards it, he took out his folding knife and sharpened his stick into a spear.

CHAPTER NINE

W hen Thorn plunged to earth, Toni followed him
down.

She found him lying, twisted up, in a tangle of white
pitcher plants. His eyes were closed, his torn wings spread,
like a giant, battered butterfly. The top half of his body was
on a cushion of moss, but he was slowly slipping off it, into
the black waters of the swamp beneath.

Toni hovered warily above Thorn, her main wings closed,
her smaller ancillary wings buzzing. She thought it was a
trap. She thought, when she got within grabbing distance,
his bright green eyes would shoot open and he'd drag her to
the ground, where she'd be helpless.

'Hey,' she called out to him. 'Hey, Venus Angel.'

The sound of her own voice, speaking English, surprised
her. It sounded eerie in this vast, lonely wilderness of
predator plants, as if it didn't belong here at all.

Thorn didn't respond. She hovered a little lower, poked
him with her toe. He didn't even twitch. Instead his body
slipped a little further into the swamp.

She stared at his limp body, bewildered. His green skin was already losing its gloss, fading in places to yellow.

'What's wrong with you?' she demanded.

She still didn't understand why he'd gone plummeting down like a stone. Why he hadn't tried to save himself. He'd fought like a warrior, with all his strength and cunning. It had been a battle between equals. She hadn't been sure who would win.

'He can't be dead,' she murmured, to herself this time. 'I don't believe it.'

Then she saw the bullet hole in his chest, right above his human heart. It was leaking a little trickle of green plant sap.

She stared at it for a long time. Then an even stranger sound came out of Toni's mouth. It was a wild, human howl of grief and despair.

Only minutes before, they'd been enemies. They'd fought a savage aerial battle over the swamplands. *But now*, she thought, *with Thorn dead, I'm the only Venus Angel left.* There was no one like her in the whole, wide world.

Toni was a Venus Angel, Viridian's creation, his idea of the perfect Verdan. But, buried deep inside her, human feelings still flickered. Viridian wouldn't have approved at all. He'd have thought, *She's a failed experiment*, and had her terminated.

Toni flew down and crouched beside Thorn. She shook his body angrily.

'Don't you dare die!' she screamed at him, as if he'd deliberately abandoned her. But his eyes didn't open. His face looked very peaceful. His mutant body seemed at rest at last.

To Toni, the loneliness felt unbearable. She stared up at the empty skies above her, the wilderness around. She hauled Thorn's body out of the water so the swamp couldn't claim it.

A buzzard, sensing death, was circling above.

Toni clasped Thorn to her and shrieked at the buzzard, 'You can't have him!' She flashed her great crimson and green wings in warning.

The buzzard, who knew a top predator when it saw one, swooped off over the forest.

Gently, Toni lowered Thorn down again onto the cushion of moss. Then she crouched by him, guarding his dead body.

CHAPTER TEN

Jay woke up, thinking only about Toni. It was his second day of walking.

You'll see her today, he promised himself.

If he walked fast, he'd reach the swamplands by late afternoon, maybe early evening.

Still half asleep, he reached out for his backpack and checked the two small plastic bottles in the front pocket. They were still there, with the precious clear liquid inside. All Toni had to do was swallow the vaccine from one bottle and her body would make antibodies to fight the virus. She'd be cured. And she'd never be able to catch it again.

She'd need an operation, of course, to get rid of those freaky grafted wings. But after that, Jay told himself, he'd have the old Toni back. She wouldn't look any different to any human girl.

Jay staggered out, from under the gorse bush where he'd spent the night. He stretched his stiff and aching body.

His head felt like it was full of cement. He had to wake himself up. He had hours of walking ahead.

Rubbing the sleep from his eyes, Jay stumbled to the river bank. The river was wide and slow-flowing. He knelt down at its edge to scoop up some cold water to splash his face. Then he cupped some in his hands and lapped it up, like a dog.

As the ripples cleared, he stared into the water. Instead of his own reflection, two glowing green eyes stared back at him, burning with hatred. He'd walked right into an ambush.

Get your weapon, Jay's brain commanded him.

He shot to his feet and sped off like a greyhound.

But the Green Vampire exploded from the river bed in a fountain of spray, his green skin glistening with oxygen bubbles. He sprang onto the bank in a panther-like crouch. He was a hulking, muscle-bound monster, far stronger than any human but still horribly springy and supple.

He took off after Jay, in long, loping strides, crashing through bracken, leaping over gorse bushes and fallen trees, covering the ground with incredible speed. Plant creepers, grafted onto his body, writhed like sinews around his arms and chest. The tips of some of them waved in sinister circles, as if sniffing the air to locate their prey.

Jay skidded to a halt by his backpack, snatched up his spear.

He spun around, his eyes hot and savage as the Immune Hunter's. Because of the fungus spreading inside him, Jay felt his death was already certain. But not yet. Not yet.

'Come on, you green freak!' screamed Jay, hurling the spear, as he'd once, in another life, chucked the javelin in games lessons at Franklin High.

He saw the spear stick, quivering between the Immune Hunter's ribs. Heard the plant/human hybrid howl with rage as he yanked it from his chest, with a spurt of green sap.

But then Jay was choking. His hands flew to his throat. A creeper had uncoiled from the Green Vampire's skin. Ten metres long, it hissed through the air like a whip. It spun twice around Jay's throat and tightened.

As it strangled him, Jay was aware there were other creepers, winding around his ankles and legs, pulling him down. He fell to his knees, fighting for breath, his chest on fire, his heart pumping desperately, trying to get blood to his brain. His fingers tore at the creepers around his neck. But they were strong as steel wires. He couldn't break them. Now, trussed up in creepers, gasping for breath, he was being dragged through the gorse bushes. The Green Vampire was reeling him in like a dying fish.

Jay's eyes went blank and glazed over. A black tidal wave came crashing into his brain...

Suddenly, the creepers slackened. Like magic, they flew off his body. Jay saw daylight again, dragged air into his scorching lungs. Then he was on all fours, throwing up. When there was nothing left in his stomach, he wiped his mouth and realized, *I'm still alive.*

He peered through the gorse bushes.

'That's so gross,' whispered Jay, flattening himself into the ground.

The hunter had been hunted. An even bigger Green Vampire had come from the forest, lured by the smell of freshly spilled plant sap. While the first Green Vampire was throttling Jay, another Green Vampire had sneaked up behind him.

Green Vampires couldn't be strangled like humans because they breathed through their chlorophyll skin. So the bigger Green Vampire had felled Jay's attacker with a mighty blow. Now he was crouching over his victim, green spit drooling from his mouth.

Jay watched the whole gruesome process from his hiding place. It was just as the sick Verdan woman had said. Creepers from the bigger Green Vampire clamped onto the unconscious vampire's body, burrowed down to his veins and began to drain him of plant sap. Like a blood transfusion, the sap was carried back through the creepers, to make the bigger Green Vampire stronger, boost his immune system.

Green Vampires would do anything to survive, even cannibalise their own kind.

Jay had only a few minutes to escape, while the monster was busy feeding. Grabbing his backpack, still on all fours, he scooted backwards through the gorse bushes. When he was at a safe distance, he stood up and ran.

It took twenty minutes for Jay to circle around and come back, further south, to the river bank. He kept checking behind him. But there were no green freaks bounding after him.

'They're not that interested in me,' Jay figured.

It was other, healthy Verdans they were hunting down now, for food, to keep them alive.

And anyhow, thought Jay, with the same crazy defiance he'd clung to since yesterday, *those vampire freaks can't kill me.*

Where Jay's death was concerned, Viridian had already staked his claim.

CHAPTER ELEVEN

The shadows were getting longer. It was mid-afternoon but still hot and sticky. Jay batted at the flies around his head. They flew away, then came back again, in a buzzing halo.

He was almost through the forest now. He was so close to the swamplands that he kept checking the sky to see if a Venus Angel was swooping up there on green and crimson wings.

He only expected to see Toni. He didn't believe that there were two of them, like some guy had told Dad.

The guy got it wrong, thought Jay. *Or he was exaggerating, like hunters do.*

As far as Jay was concerned Toni was Viridian's creation, the only one. Jay wanted it to be that way. He thought it was another reason that Toni would be desperate to take the vaccine.

'If I was the only one of something,' Jay decided, 'I'd hate it, with everybody staring, saying, *Look at that freak*. I'd want to be the same as everyone else.'

From the corner of his eye, Jay caught something moving in the grass. It was well camouflaged.

Verdan, he thought immediately. But was it an Immune Hunter?

Jay cursed himself: he hadn't got a weapon. He'd left his spear in the Green Vampire and hadn't sharpened another one.

The Verdan burst from the grass. Jay was all fired up to fight. Then he realized it was someone he knew.

'Sage!' he said, lowering his fists.

Sage was Viridian's younger sister. She was as fanatical as her big brother. When Jay last met her, back when Viridian ruled, she'd been training to be an Immune Hunter.

Viridian's empire had fallen before she made it. But it seemed she was still full of the same old hatreds.

'Filthy Polluter,' she said, furiously, green spit flying from her mouth. 'Why aren't you Verdan? Are you an Immune?' That last idea seemed to enrage her even more. 'All Immunes are terrorists. They must be terminated without mercy,' she chanted, a lesson she'd learned off by heart.

Jay said, 'Don't you remember me? I'm Jay Rainbird.'

'Then you are an Immune!' screamed Sage. It seemed that, any second, she might fly at him, try to rake out his eyes with her green nails. But something in Jay's face, maybe his complete lack of fear for his own safety, made her change her mind. 'I'm going to find an Immune Hunter. Get you arrested.'

'I wouldn't do that,' Jay warned her. 'I especially wouldn't find a Green Vampire.'

He noticed that Sage had kept herself healthy; her skin was bright green and glossy, with no plant diseases.

'I haven't seen any Green Vampires,' said Sage.

'You've been lucky then,' said Jay. 'You should stay away from them.'

'Why?' said Sage. 'They're my friends. Not like dirty Polluters.'

Jay shook his head in disbelief. Where had she been all this time? Didn't she know everything had changed and that the time of the Verdans was over?

He asked her, 'Have you been living in the forest? Don't you know what's been happening outside?'

'I'm not supposed to talk to Polluters,' said Sage, her green eyes flashing venom.

'They've found a cure,' Jay explained. 'Everyone's human again. There's hardly any Verdans like you left.'

'I don't believe you,' said Sage. 'You're just trying to trick me.' But Jay saw doubt in her eyes.

'You know don't you?' Jay said, in a gentle voice he hadn't used for a long time. 'You know it's all over.'

For a second he thought she was going to admit it. But then her eyes hardened with hate again and she snarled, 'When I'm an Immune Hunter, I'm going to get you!'

To his surprise, Jay felt a rush of pity. She was just a kid. A kid who'd been taught to spout hatred when she was too young even to understand what she was saying; a kid who still dreamt that she could be an Immune Hunter one day, with all the fame and privileges and power that used to bring, back in the days when Viridian ruled.

Did she think Viridian was dead, like most people hoped?

It was on the tip of Jay's tongue to tell her, 'Your brother is still alive.' He'd leave out the bit about him being a Fungoid; it would take too long to explain and he didn't have the time.

Then he realized that Sage wouldn't care either way. Verdans didn't care about anyone, even other Verdans. Ordinary Verdans cared about water, sunshine and minerals. Cultivars and Immune Hunters cared about power. They had the DNA of the world's most aggressive plants in their bodies. They'd ruthlessly kill any rival who got in their way.

But Sage wasn't an Immune Hunter. She never would be. She was just some poor, brainwashed child.

Jay stood there, wondering what to do.

'Come with me,' he told Sage. 'I'll protect you. This forest is a dangerous place.'

Sage said, 'I'm not going anywhere with an Immune.'

'Go on your own then,' Jay begged her, 'Go to Franklin, for the cure.'

'I don't want to be human,' said Sage. 'Humans are our enemies. They must be terminated.'

Stupid kid, thought Jay. *She deserves all she gets.* But then he thought about her, wandering alone through the forest, still believing Green Vampires were her friends. And he acted on impulse. Even as he was reaching into his backpack to get one of his precious bottles of vaccine, part of his mind was saying, *Are you crazy?*

But he ignored it. He handed the bottle to Sage and said, 'Take it. It's the cure for the plant virus. It'll make you human again.'

Sage said, 'Don't you *listen*? I don't want to be human again. Being human sucks!'

But she reached out her green hand and grabbed the bottle from him.

Jay said, 'I've got to go.' He was already regretting what he'd done. He thought he'd better get moving or he might snatch the bottle back.

Before he disappeared into the trees he looked back one last time. Sage was still clutching the bottle, staring at it.

He had no idea whether or not she would take it.

He yelled out, 'Stay lucky,' then plunged into the trees.

Sage frowned at the little plastic bottle for a long, long time, her mind pulling her this way and that. But finally, she unscrewed the top.

A rustling came from behind her. Sage spun round, dropped the bottle. Then a smile broke out all over her face.

'Hi!' she said, as the Green Vampire rose up from the gorse bushes.

Jay saw the human vigilante from a long way off. The vigilante wasn't trying to conceal himself. He came swaggering along the river bank in full view, his rifle over his shoulder. As far as he was concerned, humans had regained control. They were back in their rightful place, as masters of the planet.

'Hey,' he greeted Jay, with a friendly grin. 'How you doing?'

'You just come from the swamplands?' Jay asked him, a terrible dread already clutching his heart.

'Yeah. Just got one of those green vermin,' bragged the vigilante, bursting with pride. 'It was a Venus Angel. Shot it right out of the sky. My best shot ever. Hope they believe me back home because – '

'You stupid, murdering scumbag!' screamed Jay.

As Jay yelled abuse, bafflement and then rage crossed the vigilante's face.

'You're one of those of those green freak lovers, aren't you?' sneered the vigilante, taking his rifle from his shoulder. 'One of those crazies that talk crap like, "We mustn't wipe out an entire species." Like, "They've got a right to live." You're as bad as them!'

But Jay was already gone, sprinting away from the river bank. He plunged back into the shadowy forest, zig-zagging between trees, so, if the vigilante decided to bring him down, he couldn't get a clear shot.

CHAPTER TWELVE

J ay came sprinting out of the trees.

She might just be injured, he was telling himself, hoping against hope. *The hunter said he'd shot her down. He never* definitely *said he'd killed her.*

The swamplands stretched into the hazy distance. Vast plains of sticky sundews glinting like rubies, Venus fly traps and tall, ghostly pitchers. Between the islands of plants, great rafts of bright green moss floated on black swamp water.

'Toni!' yelled Jay, looking frantically around, dreading what he might find.

The hum of flies rose from the swamp like drowsy music. But those trapped in the plants and being slowly dissolved made a high-pitched, tormented whining that went on and on and on.

Jay saw spectacular wings, flapping like a giant bird of prey. Then a Venus Angel rose slowly from the swamp.

'Toni?' whispered Jay, hardly believing what he saw.

His stunned gaze followed the plant/human mutant as it rose. He'd forgotten just how freaky, how awesome she was.

Her hair had grown out of its spiky clumps. Now it wafted in green curls around her head. Her shorts and top were tattered. But it was Toni all right. Who else could it be? She was the only Venus Angel in the world.

Jay, delirious with joy and relief, let out a great whoop. He leapt up, punched his fist in the air. Yes! She was alive.

'Hey, Toni!' he yelled.

She was alive. She didn't even seem hurt. That lying vigilante! Jay laughed out loud. That creep was either a liar, or a really bad shot.

'Hey, Toni,' he yelled again. 'It's me, Jay. Told you I'd find you!'

He raced right to the edge of the black swamp water, fumbling in his backpack for the cure that would change Toni back into a human girl.

He held his one precious vaccine bottle up high. She came swooping down to meet him. He heard the rackety sound of her great, beating wings, saw water droplets gleam on her glossy green skin.

Then he saw her eyes, full of fury and pain.

Toni attacked, screeching, her long sharp nails trying to rake out his eyes. The tiny bottle flew out of his hand and was lost in the water. Jay shielded his eyes with his arms, stumbling blindly about, as she darted around him, trying to get to his face, or trap his limbs in her spiky wings. A great wing blow slammed him off balance, made him stagger into the swamp. At first, he didn't sink. But then the moss raft he'd stepped on wobbled, once, twice. Suddenly it sank under his weight and he plunged with it into the bog beneath.

And then there was silence, except for the buzz and whine of flies. Jay's brain, numb with shock, took a while to grasp his situation. He was standing knee deep in water, made soupy by the husks of flies the plants had sucked dry and spat out.

Toni wasn't far away. A dead tree stuck out of the swamp and she was perched in its white, skeleton branches. Her great wings were folded. She seemed to be waiting.

Jay's brain started working again. And his first thought was, *She didn't mean to attack me*. It had all been a misunderstanding.

'Toni, it's me, Jay,' he called out. 'I'm on your side. It was us against Viridian, remember. Me and you. Look, I brought you the vaccine.'

Jay looked at his hand and realised it was empty. Then he realised something else too. When he tried to wade towards Toni, he couldn't. Somewhere under that water, his feet were cemented in mud. He tried to tug them free. They were stuck fast. With a sudden, sick lurch, he sank further, up to his thighs.

This can't be happening, he thought. *I'm not supposed to die now in some stinking swamp.*

And suddenly the fighting spirit that had fired him up throughout the journey went stone cold.

He started to panic then, struggling to free himself. But the swamp pulled him further in.

Toni watched from her tree, with that intense, unblinking predator's stare. She saw Jay sink to his waist.

She'd stopped attacking him because it was a waste of energy. She knew that he was no danger. He didn't have a gun. And now the swamp had got him, he was doomed.

She should have dismissed him from her mind, flown back to guard Thorn's body. But Thorn was safe, for the moment, hidden from buzzards by heaps of pitcher plant traps that she'd piled upon him, like white funeral lilies.

She heard Jay scream, 'Help me, Toni!'

Still she didn't move from her perch.

But flashbacks were troubling her mind; flashbacks from when she'd been human. Desperately, she tried to deny them. Still they came sneaking back.

She barely thought in words any more. But, in her head, she saw, vivid as if it had only just happened, Jay hacking off her hair with his dad's kitchen scissors, saving her from the Immune Hunter.

Then she pictured him, far away on the ground, a tiny, pathetic human figure, as she'd soared off into the night, to start her new life, here in the swamplands.

And suddenly, something was touched in her human heart. Venus Angels should hate humans, hunt them down, without mercy. And, after they'd killed Thorn, Toni had even more cause. But, somehow, she cared about this one.

She pitied him too. Poor Jay, imprisoned in his human body. He would never have her powers, or know what flying felt like.

'Jay!' she called out. 'Stay still and you won't sink.'

But Jay didn't seem to be listening. His next cry for help was near-hysterical.

'Toni! Do something!'

Toni pictured him in her mind, disappearing under foul swamp water, coming up fighting for air, then being pulled down one final time. She pictured the ripples smoothing, as if Jay had never existed. She'd seen deer drown in the swamp when they'd strayed onto a moss raft, thinking it was solid ground. If she didn't help him, the same thing would happen to Jay. She pictured his death struggles...

'No!' she cried, out loud, horrified. She couldn't bear those images.

She left the tree and flew to his rescue.

Jay heard her swooshing wings, saw her flying over the swamp towards him.

He shielded his face with his arms. But this time she didn't attack. Instead she swooped downward and clamped her green fingers around his wrists.

'Stay still,' she ordered him again. And this time Jay listened. It had penetrated even his panicking brain that she wasn't going to harm him; that she meant to help him.

Her grip was vice-like. Venus Angels, created to be Viridian's supreme warriors and personal bodyguard, were stronger than Green Vampires. But even for a Venus Angel, it was a tough job to pull Jay free, to make the swamp mud surrender him. Toni's main wings clapped above them both with slow, powerful beats while the small ancillary wings on her wrists and ankles buzzed frantically to give her maximum lift.

Jay stared, hypnotized, into her glinting green eyes as she hovered above him. But all he saw there was fierce determination, as she fought to get him free.

'Help me, Jay,' said Toni.

And Jay, waking out of his daze, gripped her wrists with his hands to make the bond between them stronger. Suddenly, he could kick his legs.

'I'm coming out!' he yelled at Toni.

Then, with one massive tug, she yanked him free. She couldn't fly far with Jay as a dead weight dangling beneath her. Her face was contorted with the effort, her body slick and shiny with the water that transpired from her chlorophyll skin. But it was only a few mighty wing flaps before she could get rid of her burden and dump him on the grass at the swamp's edge.

Jay lay there, where she'd let him fall, trying to get his head around what had just happened.

She rescued you, you dummy, he told himself. That meant she still had feelings for him, that she wanted them to be together.

He staggered to his feet, elation flooding through him.

Dad had said, 'Give her up. She won't be missing you. She won't even remember who you are.'

Dr Moran had said, 'She won't want to be cured. She's so far from human now, it would be cruel to try.'

Well, they were both wrong, Jay told himself. *I never believed them anyway.*

But black thoughts that he'd buried deep during the journey came sneaking back into his brain, trying to spoil his happiness.

There were so many things Toni didn't know. She didn't know Viridian was still alive. That her mother Teal had died, executed on Viridian's command, in the Etiolation Cave. Or that Jay had breathed in Viridian's Earthstar spores that even now were probably growing inside him, killing him, slowly...

He couldn't deal with any of that now. He'd found Toni alive hadn't he? And she still cared about him. What else mattered? All that other stuff hardly seemed real anyhow, not out here in the swamplands. Maybe it would when they were back in Franklin and Toni was human again.

'Hey, Toni,' he yelled out. 'Doesn't matter about losing that vaccine bottle. There's plenty more back in Franklin.'

Jay gazed out over the swamplands, that weird, whining, killing ground of beautiful carnivorous plants. It seemed like Franklin was light years away.

He shivered, suddenly chilled, as if a cloud had covered the sun. But the sun was as bright and hot as ever.

Where's Toni gone? he thought, anxiously. He shaded his eyes against the glare as he searched the swamplands for her. Then he found her again, quite close.

His heart leapt again with relief. She'd stayed around. He'd thought for one terrible second that she'd flown off again and left him.

She'd blended into the greenery on a plant island. That was why he didn't spot her straightaway. But suddenly she slid out, into the sunshine.

'Hey, Toni?' Jay yelled. 'We'd better get a move on, back to Franklin.' *The sooner she's human the better*, thought Jay. He suddenly wanted to get far away from this creepy place.

But Toni ignored him, as if he didn't exist. She'd rescued him; she didn't even know why. He was on his own now. She was done with humans.

Jay waved like crazy. 'Toni, you coming?'

He saw her great wings were spread, shading something from the sun. What was it? Jay couldn't get a clear view. It seemed to be a heap of white lilies.

Toni squatted back on her heels. She folded her wings, like the stone angels carved on tombs. And now Jay could see everything. Tenderly, Toni leaned forward and brushed aside some of the flowers.

What's she doing? thought Jay, doubt and dread already creeping into his mind.

Then Toni lifted up the limp body of another Venus Angel and hugged him to her chest, gazing round fiercely with those alien eyes. As if she was thinking, *Don't even try to take him from me.*

Jay's mind was swirling in a sea of confusion. At first, his traumatized brain just couldn't make sense of what he saw.

'I thought she was the only one,' he whispered, bewildered.

He hadn't believed Dad's story, about vigilantes seeing more than one Venus Angel. But now he had to believe it, because he was looking at two of them, with his own eyes.

They were near enough for Jay to make out the other Venus Angel's face. Jay recognised it, despite the chlorophyll skin. At school, right from when he was four years old, he'd seen that face every day.

'Mac,' murmured Jay.

Mac, who had once been the class clown, always cheery, cracking jokes, who'd become Thorn, Viridian's fanatical follower, and then, somehow, a Venus Angel. His skin was fading to yellow, as Verdan skin did when they'd died.

So the trigger-happy hunter hadn't lied either. He *had* shot a Venus Angel out of the sky. But it was Thorn, not Toni.

And Toni was grieving over him, as if she truly missed him.

A stab of jealousy shot through Jay, as if Toni had somehow betrayed him.

Then he told himself, *Cool down. Maybe it's not like it looks.*

His mind was thrown into chaos again. Then, behind him in the forest, he heard an engine rev hard and tyres skidding on the dirt track.

Jay whirled round. Was it that hunter coming back, with transport this time and some of his bloodthirsty vigilante mates?

Jay saw bull bars smash through the trees, with battered teddies tied to them. He saw a familiar face through the mud-smeared windscreen.

'Dad!' said Jay, as the truck screeched to a stop beside him.

CHAPTER THIRTEEN

'I got fuel,' said Dad, proudly, as he leapt from the driving seat. 'So I followed you here. What on earth happened to you? Looks like you fell in the swamp. Where's your other shoe?'

Jay looked down at his sodden, mud-caked sock and, for the first time realised that when Toni had pulled him out, he'd left one of his trainers behind.

'Did you find her?' asked Dad, scanning the swamp. Then his jaw went slack with amazement. 'Is that *her*?'

Jay followed Dad's gaze. 'Yeah,' he said.

Toni had covered Thorn's corpse again and was sitting perched in the branches of the dead tree. Her wings were open, ready for take-off, and her green eyes blazed with fury at yet another human intruder on her territory.

Dad shaded his eyes, so he could see her better.

'I've never seen anything like that in my whole life,' he whispered, shaking his head in disbelief.

And then Jay remembered that Dad had never seen Toni, not even as a human girl and certainly not as a Venus Angel.

'I've seen those Immune Hunters, those Green Vampires even. But her!' Dad's voice was filled with awe and repulsion. 'Just what kind of monster is she?'

Jay opened his mouth to protest, 'She's not a monster,' but Dad was already apologizing. 'Look, I'm sorry son, I know she means a lot to you. It's just a shock. I mean, I didn't expect her to be so, so...' Dad stopped, clearly scared he was going to say something even more unforgivable. He started again, like he was trying to reassure himself. 'But she'll be all right, won't she, when she takes the cure? Even like she is. I mean, those wings on her back, they can be cut off, can't they? Like, she'll have scars, probably, but she can wear a T-shirt or something and she'll forget all this, in time and...'

'Shut up, Dad and get in the truck,' Jay interrupted urgently. 'I think she's going to attack.' He could see the warning signs. Toni was beating her wings, flashing the green and red insides like a threat. Now she was rising effortlessly from the tree.

Dad had already jumped inside. 'What are you waiting for?' he was yelling at Jay. 'Get in!'

For a few frantic seconds, Jay argued with himself. *Why are you taking cover? She's not going to hurt you.*

But he wasn't at all sure about that, and when Toni came streaking over the swamp, shrieking like a hawk, Jay ran and jumped into the truck cab beside Dad. 'Get your arm inside, Dad,' he said, breathlessly. 'Close the windows. Or she'll trap your arm in her wings and you'll never get it out.'

Jay didn't add that her wings had spikes and digestive juices that could dissolve your flesh. Dad was already freaked out, shaking like a leaf. He'd started up the engine.

'Wait a minute,' said Jay.

'Are you insane?' said Dad. 'We've got to get out of here.'

'Wait,' repeated Jay, calmly reaching over and turning the key to switch the engine off. 'Wait a minute.'

Jay had steeled himself for Toni flying round the truck, going berserk as she had before, maybe smashing it with wing blows, trying to find a way in, shattering the windscreen with her fists or feet.

But she wasn't doing that.

Jay and Dad sat in the silence. Jay batted off a fat bluebottle that had taken refuge in the truck from the carnivorous plants.

Finally Dad said, 'Where is she?'

Jay looked through the window, checked in the wing mirror. 'She's in the back of the truck,' he said wonderingly. 'Just sitting there.'

'Then she wants a ride back to Franklin with us,' said Dad. 'So she can get the cure. You don't have any vaccine with you, do you?'

'I did,' said Jay. 'But I lost it.'

'Then let's take her back,' said Dad, reaching out again to start up the engine. 'Sooner the better.'

'She won't go back, Dad.' Jay frowned. 'She won't co-operate. You start that engine, she'll fly back into the swamp.'

'How'd you know that?' demanded Dad.

Jay was doing some rapid thinking. He could have told Dad how he knew that. It was because he'd just seen Toni with Thorn, another Venus Angel, protecting his body, hugging him to her, as if she'd lost part of herself. Jay thought, *She'll never leave this place.*

But Jay didn't let on about Thorn. Because a voice in his head was arguing, *Maybe Dad's right.* Once she got back to Franklin, took the cure, maybe she'd forget about Thorn and the swamplands, forget she was ever a Venus Angel.

'How'd you know she won't come willingly?' asked Dad again.

'I just do,' said Jay. 'I think she'll fight us every step of the way. Maybe she doesn't even remember she's supposed to be human. Maybe she thinks she was *born* a Venus Angel. Who knows what she thinks?'

Strangely, that seemed to satisfy Dad. He nodded in agreement, his jaw clenched in that stubborn way Jay knew so well. 'OK, then. We need to tie her down or something. Stop her flying away somehow. Then we get her back to Franklin ASAP. It's for her own good,' said Dad. 'When she's human again, she'll thank us.'

And Jay so desperately wanted to believe that, to carry on clinging to his dream, that he found himself replying, 'Yeah, Dad. I bet she will.'

'So let's do it,' said Dad. He gave Jay a sudden, wary grin. 'You obviously know more about 'em than I do. How do you catch a Venus Angel?'

'What have you got in this truck?' asked Jay.

Dad shrugged, 'A lot of junk. There's some gear in the back, rods and stuff. He must've been a fisherman, the guy who had this truck before me.'

For a moment Jay had some wild idea about casting a rod like anglers do, hooking Toni in mid-air, maybe in a wing – a hook in her wing wouldn't hurt her too much. Then you could reel her in like a fish. But immediately he thought, *No way*. He'd seen what a fighter she was. No rod would be strong enough to hold her. She'd just rip the hook out, probably not even notice, as she soared up into the sky.

'There's an old net,' said Dad. 'It's full of holes. But maybe if we could sneak up...'

'No chance, Dad,' said Jay. 'You can't sneak up on a Venus Angel. She's on the look-out all the time. She doesn't trust humans.'

'She trusts you,' said Dad.

'She's taking off,' said Jay, as he heard the beating of wings and checked in the mirror.

Dad frowned. 'Where's she going?'

Toni didn't go back to Thorn, not while they were still around. Instead, she sat in her dead tree, far out of reach, in the swamp.

'So what do we do now?' said Dad.

'I don't know,' said Jay. 'I'm thinking.'

Toni didn't know what to do either. She should be attacking now, driving out the invaders. But those memories

94

of Jay somehow prevented her. She screamed with rage and rocked her head back and forth. But she couldn't shake them out of her mind.

So she just sat in her tree, waiting for them to leave.

Like any top predator, Toni had endless patience. She could sit still for hours. While she waited, she inspected her foot, the one Thorn had injured two days before. His spiky wings had made deep puncture wounds. But Venus Angels were fast healing. Already the holes had skinned over. Soon there'd be a row of little bumps, like tribal tattoos, to show where they'd been.

Toni smiled proudly. They were her first battle scars.

Every so often her fierce gaze swept the sky. She was searching for buzzards. Those, she'd attack instantly. But none came swooping over the swamplands. And Thorn was well hidden, under the pitcher plants she'd piled there to hide his body and to honour him.

'I've thought of something,' Jay told Dad. 'We can catch her, maybe even with a net. But we've got to slow her down first, make her weak, so she doesn't attack us or fly away.'

'And just how do you propose to do that?' asked Dad, sceptically.

'Toni told me something, back when she was human. She told me about Venus fly traps.'

'That what you two talked about? Carnivorous plants? You sure this girl wasn't weird even when she was human?'

'Shut up, Dad! You don't know anything about Toni.'

Dad seemed shocked at Jay's furious response. 'Sorry,' he said. 'I didn't mean to make you mad. I know what this girl means to you...'

'Forget it,' Jay muttered.

'I'll keep my big mouth shut from now on,' promised Dad. 'So what did Toni tell you?'

'She told me you mustn't keep triggering their traps. Because they get weaker, they lose all their energy. Toni's got giant Venus fly traps for wings – '

'You're saying it would be the same with her?' Dad interrupted. 'That she'd get weak, like it would ground her, she wouldn't be able to take off?'

'I don't know,' confessed Jay. 'I don't know if it would work with Venus Angels.'

But Dad was enthusiastic, as if he'd bought into Jay's idea. 'It's worth trying. So how do we trigger her wings?'

'We throw something between them, so they snap shut. They have these hairs inside that get triggered electrically.'

'So what do we throw exactly?' asked Dad.

'I dunno.' Jay shrugged. 'Something soft that won't hurt her. Is there anything like that in the truck?'

Dad was shaking his head. 'Don't think so.' He paused. 'What about the bears?'

'What bears? What are you talking about?' Then Jay remembered the soft toys strapped to the bull bars. He screwed up his face for a few seconds, thinking, and decided, 'That might work.'

'I'll cut a few loose,' said Dad.

'No, I will,' said Jay. 'You can't go out there. She'll attack you.'

'Be careful,' said Dad. 'I heard those Venus Angels fight to the death.'

'Yeah,' said Jay. 'They do.'

But he didn't feel scared for his personal safety. He didn't even give it a thought. Viridian had already infected him with lethal spores that sooner or later would kill him. What could Toni do that was worse than that?

He felt in his jeans pocket for his folding knife. It wasn't there. He'd lost it somewhere, maybe when he was struggling in the swamp.

'Have you got anything I can cut with?' he asked Dad.

'There's an angling knife here,' said Dad, handing it to him. 'For gutting fish. Watch out, it's razor sharp.'

Jay opened the truck door. 'Wait a minute,' said Dad. 'How are you planning to do this? How can you trigger her wings? She's too far away. Can you can throw that far?'

Jay privately thought, *No, I can't*. But he climbed out and shut the door on Dad's worried questions. Then he turned back and tapped on the window. Dad slid it part way down.

'Stay inside, Dad,' Jay said, through the gap. 'She'll just get mad again if she sees you. She doesn't like humans.'

CHAPTER FOURTEEN

Jay crouched, keeping low, by the front of the truck. Out of sight of Toni, he slashed a teddy bear off the bull bars. This bear wasn't cute any more. No child would want him to cuddle. He was a filthy lump of fur with a leg missing, barely recognisable as a bear at all.

Jay slashed three more teddies free, while Dad watched anxiously from inside the cab. Then, with one bear hidden behind his back, tucked into the belt of his jeans, Jay came round the front of the truck, where Toni could see him. On the way, he threw the sharp angling knife into the open back.

Jay stood at the edge of the swamp, arms spread out at his sides, hands open, as if to say, 'Look, I've got no weapons.'

Toni watched him curiously from her tree. But she didn't come any closer.

'Toni!' Jay yelled out, over the swamp. 'I'm leaving. I'm getting in the truck now. I'm going back to Franklin. Stay lucky. Have a good life.'

Toni waited. When Jay left, that would end the confusion inside her head. He would go back to his world, where he belonged. She would stay here in hers. A sudden disturbing image came into her head. It was of herself, swooping over her territory, queen of the swamplands, free, but all alone in an endless, empty sky.

She was driving that picture from her mind with some particularly savage head-shaking when Jay yelled out again. 'Aren't you coming to say goodbye?'

Still Toni didn't move.

Jay thought, *This isn't going to work.*

Then, suddenly, she rose from her tree. Was she going back to guard Thorn's body? No, she wasn't. She came drifting over the swamp towards Jay on majestic, slow-flapping wings.

Jay let out a long breath. Behind his back, he pulled the bear from his belt. He had to get this right. He only had one chance.

She didn't land. On the ground, Venus Angels are at a big disadvantage. Jay saw suspicion in her green, glinting eyes. It seemed she didn't trust humans, not even him.

And she was right not to trust him. He was telling her lies, tricking her into coming closer. And he was about to do far worse than that. He thought, *Am I doing the right thing?* But he reassured himself, echoing Dad's words: 'It's for her own good.' When she was human again, back in Franklin, she'd forgive him.

Jay really wanted to believe that.

'Bye,' said Toni, awkwardly.

She couldn't think what else to say. She hardly used his language any more.

But, looking down at him, anchored to the earth, as she hovered above in mid-air, it was suddenly clear they were worlds apart. She should never have doubted what she'd believed before – that there was no future for her with humans. Not even with Jay, who seemed different from all the rest. She was a warrior angel with her first battle scars. Where would Jay fit into her life?

'Bye,' said Toni again. This time there was finality in her voice.

'Bye,' said Jay, struggling not to let his tension show.

Toni was swooping away, when Jay threw the first bear, aiming it right between her wings. Instantly, they clamped shut.

Jay dashed back behind the truck, snatched up the other bear missiles.

Toni gazed after him, bewildered. She had no idea what he was doing. But she was too busy trying to stay airborne to think, her ancillary wings buzzing like frantic bees. And she could have managed it, flown to a place of safety, but her predator plant instincts were over-riding her human brain. They gave her main wings the message: *This isn't something to eat*. Her wings instantly opened and dropped the bear.

But before she could soar away, Jay was back. He threw another mangled fur ball into her main wings. They clapped shut around it in a fraction of a second, faster than the human eye could follow.

As they opened again to spit out the useless bear. Jay chucked another. He could hardly miss now because Toni was coming lower. The huge electrical surges, opening and closing her wings in such quick succession, were a massive shock to her body. Her bare green toes were almost touching the ground. She struggled to take off again but she was swaying, her head drooping on her chest.

When her wings opened again, Jay had another missile ready. But he didn't throw it.

Toni herself had told him that too much triggering could kill Venus fly traps. Did that apply to plant/human hybrids? And how much triggering was too much? A hundred times? As few as three or four? Jay couldn't take the risk. Even if it meant she escaped.

But it seemed Toni was already earthbound, vulnerable. Even with open wings, she couldn't take off. She staggered around, then fell to her knees. But she wouldn't give up. She crawled, her wings dragging, like a giant injured bat.

Jay couldn't bear it, seeing a great Venus Angel reduced to such a pathetic state. He asked himself, horrified, *What have you done to her?* He went running over, tried to help her.

As he struggled to lift her, her foot scraped a sharp stone, opening those almost healed puncture wounds. Green sap began to trickle out of them, over her toes.

Toni didn't notice, because she'd suddenly slumped in Jay's arms. She was a dead weight. He couldn't hold her, so he lowered her carefully onto the grass. She lay curled up, her eyes closed.

Jay dropped to his knees beside her, his heart pounding in panic. Was she alive?

How did you tell with a Venus Angel?

The he saw her tiny ancillary wings quivering, vainly trying to lift up her limp body. He pulled up an eyelid and saw her green eyes, still bright, still twitching with life.

Now Dad was beside him. 'Is she all right?'

'Yeah, I think so,' said Jay. 'But she might wake up soon.'

Jay could imagine her, as soon as her energy levels rose, exploding into the sky and freedom.

'Then we've got to move fast,' said Dad. 'I'll get the net.' As he rummaged in the back of the truck, he said to Jay. 'Good work, son. You were brilliant.'

Jay, kneeling by Toni's body, his head bowed, said nothing.

They wrapped Tony in the net, her wings pinioned, so even if she woke, she couldn't take off. With Jay anxiously running alongside, Dad carried her and gently laid her in the open back of the truck.

'I'll ride in the back with her,' said Jay, jumping in.

Dad didn't argue. He just strode back to the cab, started the engine. He wanted to get away from this creepy swamp and out of the forest before nightfall.

Dad gunned the engine and the truck shot forward. Jay took one last look at the swamplands, his eyes drawn back to the place where Thorn lay, buried under pitcher plants.

And then they were in the forest and he couldn't see the swamp any more.

Jay checked that Toni was OK. She seemed fine, in a deep, peaceful sleep, recharging her energy. He brushed some strands of green hair off her face. All of her body, except her head, was rolled up in a net bundle. Jay didn't like to see her that way. And he'd been the one who'd deceived her, lured her into a trap, brought her down...

He heard a crashing sound in the forest. His head shot up.

There was something moving, through the trees behind them. Jay squinted, trying to make it out. It couldn't be human; it was too big. It blended into the greenery. Then it sprang out, onto the dirt track.

'Dad!' screamed Jay. 'Go faster!'

'What?' Dad wound down the cab windows.

'Get moving!' screamed Jay. 'There's a Green Vampire after us. It wants Toni!'

It was the Green Vampire who had killed Jay's attacker and Sage. But he was even more monstrous and menacing. Fresh infusions of plant sap had given him extra strength, swelled his muscles, made more creepers, like serpents, sprout from his green, glossy skin. And the questing tips of those creepers had smelled the plant sap that was still leaking from Toni's foot. They writhed excitedly. Their

103

chemical sense told them this plant sap was healthy and of a very superior quality.

'Drive, Dad!' yelled Jay, as the Green Vampire began to bound after the truck in great ground-swallowing strides.

Dad took one shocked look in the mirror and pressed the accelerator pedal to the floor. The tyres squealed and sent up sprays of dirt. The truck bounced and jolted.

In the open back, Jay threw himself over Toni's bundled-up, unconscious body so she didn't roll around and get hurt.

'He's still behind us!' shouted Jay.

'I can see that!' Dad screamed back, as he wrestled with the wheel, trying to stop them swerving off into a tree.

The Green Vampire was pounding down the track after them, his arms and legs pumping, his green eyes fixed on them like twin laser beams. Unlike Toni, he was a completely successful experiment. He was no longer troubled by human emotions. He was driven by instincts. And his instincts told him: hunt, kill, feed. Sometimes he fed when his prey was still alive. Either way, he didn't mind.

But even for a Green Vampire, it was an incredible feat to outrun a vehicle going flat out.

Maybe… thought Jay. *Maybe we're going to make it.*

Then the first creeper tip reached the truck. Its other end was rooted into the Green Vampire's chest. It uncoiled as it came streaking, bullet-fast, through the air. Before Jay could react, the tip circled, sniffing around, then wormed through the net meshes and clamped onto Toni's leg. Its next move would be to burrow in, find a vein, and start transferring her nutrients along its long, whippy length to the Green Vampire's body.

'No!' screamed Jay, appalled.

He dived for the angling knife, rolled back as the truck bounced around, and slashed manically at the creeper, his face a mask of rage and disgust. The creeper was super tough, but this knife was sharp enough to slice it through. Then more creepers came whipping in, writhing around him, trying to get to Toni. Jay hacked and slashed in a mad fury. Bits of creeper fell off the truck and littered the track, still squirming. But it was like dealing with a multi-headed monster that sprouted new heads soon as you lopped one off.

If a creeper coiled around Jay's throat, he was finished. But, this time, the creepers weren't sent to kill humans. They were sent to suck food from a Venus Angel. The Green Vampire was so greedy for Toni's plant sap that green spit foamed from his jaws like a rabid dog. And, all the time, he was gaining on the truck.

'Dad!' yelled Jay, desperately.

Dad off-roaded and did a handbrake turn round a tree. Jay smelled burnt rubber and was slammed into the truck side. The knife flew out of his hand and was lost in the bracken.

While the rattling truck bucked and jolted and threw him around, Jay fought to crawl back to Toni, ready to wrench the creepers off her with his bare hands.

But there were no creepers crawling over the net. They'd been yanked off when Dad had done that tight spin around the tree. No more came sizzling through the air. The Green Vampire had reeled them back in until he sighted his prey again.

Which could be any second now, Jay reckoned. He could hear him, chasing after them, smashing down anything that got in his way.

Dad had bumped back onto the track and was powering along, pushing that old truck as hard as he could. Hanging onto Toni, Jay dared to look back.

The vampire wasn't behind them. Jay checked the forest on either side. It was still and peaceful, striped with late afternoon sun and shadow. There was no green monster crashing between the trees.

'Dad!' yelled Jay above the roaring engine. 'Think we lost him!'

Dad didn't cut his speed. He still drove like they were being pursued. He didn't slow down until they were out of the forest.

CHAPTER FIFTEEN

D ad was driving now along a wide, empty motorway. It was still a bumpy ride because of the potholes and cracked tarmac. But he could relax a little, drive more slowly. There was no-one hunting them down. They were safe enough, for the moment.

So long as Viridian's empire didn't already extend this far.

Nah, thought Dad, as he drove on, in the dying light. They were still twenty miles from Franklin. Surely even Viridian's zombie slaves couldn't have tunnelled this far with only picks and shovels?

But still Dad found himself checking the largest holes, the ones big enough for a truck to plunge into, and driving carefully round them.

Then he shuddered. He was thinking about two days ago, before he'd got a tankful of fuel and driven after Jay. When Dr Moran had almost been dragged underground, right outside the basement of Franklin High.

We had a fight on our hands, thought Dad grimly.

Those Fungoid freaks looked like the walking dead, but they were strong and they fought like wild dogs. If Dad and some other Franklin citizens hadn't come by just then, Dr Moran would have been a zombie slave himself.

'I want one alive,' Dr Moran had gasped, as his rescuers prised white, twiggy fingers from around his ankles, then pulled a howling slave from the hole.

Suddenly Dad saw a crack in the tarmac, as if an earthquake had happened, stretching right across the motorway.

Better drive round that that, he thought, whistling, as he went off road again and smashed a route through a field of tall purple thistles.

In the back of the truck, Toni slept on, building up her energy. Slumped beside her, Jay felt like he was falling apart. He felt like he was dying.

You are dying, he reminded himself.

For a short time, on the journey, he'd held off the horrors. But after the adrenalin rush of saving Toni came an adrenalin slump. Those horrors were back, squatting in his mind like hideous goblins. And this time, they were there to stay.

Jay was feverish one minute; the next chills shook his body. He felt sick, half-crazy with fear.

It's started, he told himself, trembling. Viridian's fungus had finally taken hold. Jay was coughing now. He could almost imagine it, that white fungus fuzz creeping into his lungs, blocking his arteries, spreading through his body into his brain.

'Dad!' yelled Jay. 'Stop the truck! I want to throw up!'

Dad skidded to a stop on the motorway verge. He leapt out the cab at the same time as Jay staggered from the back, with a deathly white face, hugging his shaking body with both arms.

Dad said, 'You look terrible. Are you going to throw up?'

'I don't think so,' said Jay, after a while.

'You sure? Then get in the cab beside me,' said Dad.

'What about Toni?'

Dad jumped in the back and checked Toni, still cocooned in the fishing net.

'She'll be all right back here on her own for a while. She's sleeping like a baby.'

'Can't we take that net off her?' asked Jay. 'It's like she's our prisoner.'

'Better not,' cautioned Dad. 'Not until we get back to Franklin. What if she wakes up? She'll be all confused. She won't know we're doing what's best, taking her to be cured. She could go flying back to the swamp. And I'm not driving back through that forest a second time. That'd really be pushing our luck. Besides, we've only just got enough fuel to get back to Franklin.'

Jay just nodded. He didn't have the energy to argue. He didn't have any fight left in him. He felt so weak and helpless, he could barely crawl into the cab.

I didn't think it would happen this fast, he was thinking. He'd thought he and Toni would have time together, after she'd been cured. But he could feel his body going numb, as if the fungus was shutting it down, bit by bit.

'You need some sleep, son,' said Dad, as he climbed into the cab beside Jay. 'That's all that's wrong with you. Don't worry. It'll all work out.'

He started up the truck engine.

With his last strength, Jay said, 'Work out? What planet are you on, Dad?'

Dad heard the fear and bitter fury in Jay's voice. He switched off the engine, turned round, surprised, to face him.

'I meant between you and Toni,' he said.

'How can it work out?' Jay raved, his face twisted in anguish. He felt like he was going insane; words were spilling out of his mouth but he hardly knew what they were. 'There are so many things she doesn't know. She doesn't know about Viridian being alive. She doesn't know her mum's dead. And who's going to tell her? 'Cos I can't. 'Cos I'm not going to be here.'

'Not going to be here?' said Dad, bewildered. 'Why?'

''Cos I'm dying, aren't I, stupid!' Jay shouted. Then he collapsed back into his seat and closed his eyes.

'What?' said Dad, shocked to the core.

'I'm dying from the fungus,' said Jay, his eyes still shut. He'd said it out loud, at last. He felt hot tears pouring down his face. He didn't even have the strength to wipe them away.

There was silence in the cab for a minute.

Then Dad spoke. Somehow he managed to keep his voice cool and steady. 'You're not going to die,' he said.

Jay didn't respond.

Dad asked, 'How long have you believed that? That the fungus was going to kill you? Open your eyes, look at me.'

Jay opened his eyes. 'Since Dr Moran said it wasn't,' he whispered. 'I didn't believe him. I knew he was lying.'

'He wasn't lying,' said Dad.

He handed Jay a tissue to dry his face. 'It's just the way scientists talk. Nothing's ever certain until they've got proof. He didn't have it then. But now he does.'

Again Jay didn't respond. He seemed to have gone back into a trance.

Dad said, 'Jay? Are you listening to what I've been saying?'

Jay was listening – but he still didn't dare hope. He told himself, 'Maybe this conversation is all a dream. Maybe I'm going to wake up in a minute.'

He pinched himself with jagged, dirty fingernails. It was so vicious it drew blood.

Ow, he thought, licking the wound on his forearm. At least he knew he was awake. He asked Dad, 'What proof has Dr Moran got?'

'Cast iron,' said Dad. 'Would you believe it, this Fungoid freak tried to snatch him – came up out a hole right outside the basement door. We grabbed the freak before he got Dr Moran. And it turns out he was one of the first people snatched off the street. He's been down there for months, breathing in spores. So the scanner's working again at the hospital – '

'Get to the point, Dad,' begged Jay.

'The point is – they scanned the guy. And the spores aren't growing fungus inside him. He's totally, a hundred per cent, fungus-free. Those spores *definitely* don't grow any killer fungus inside you.'

'You telling me the truth?' said Jay.

'For God's sake,' said Dad, finally exasperated. 'Do you think I'd lie about something like that? You're not going to die. Get used to it.'

Jay settled back in his seat. A deep calm washed over him. *You're not going to die*, he told himself. *You and Toni have got a future together now.*

But he was too shattered, physically and mentally, to chase that thought any further.

Jay's eyes drooped, but something was digging into the small of his back. Half asleep, his hand searched for what it was. It was one of the tattered soft toys that he'd used to capture Toni. He clutched it like a little kid clutches his teddy bear for comfort at night, and, at last, he slipped into unconsciousness.

CHAPTER SIXTEEN

Jay dragged himself, painfully, out of a deep sleep. Finally he opened his eyes.

Where am I? he thought. At first, he had no idea. There was a narrow window, part open, high up near the ceiling. He blinked in the sunlight that came spilling in over his face. He gazed, puzzled, around him, at the fat metal pipe that came in through one wall, ran over the concrete floor, and out through the opposite wall.

He wondered vaguely, *Why are those crates stacked in a corner?*

Then it suddenly hit him: *You're back in Franklin.*

He was in a storage room in the basement of Franklin High School. He was lying on the iron cot that had been his makeshift bed ever since he and Dad moved in here.

Thoughts came rushing in, too fast for him to deal with. So he concentrated on two: *You're not going to die. You got Toni back safe from the swamplands.*

Jay leapt out of bed. He needed to find her. He supposed she was somewhere here, in the basement.

He remembered everything now: throwing the toy bears into Toni's wings, netting her like a fish. He remembered Dad telling him that incredible news in the cab: 'You're not going to die.'

His whole world looked different now, bright and full of possibilities. Someone had left some clean clothes by his bed. Eagerly, Jay pulled them on. He couldn't wait to see Toni. How long had he slept? Maybe hours, maybe even for a whole day. Toni must have taken the vaccine by now. She'd be almost human again, apart from her wings. And that could be fixed, no problem.

Other thoughts prowled, like circling wolves, in the dark at the back of Jay's mind. What about all the things Toni didn't know? She didn't know Viridian was still alive and much more powerful than before: Viridian who'd made her become a Venus Angel; who'd had her mother executed. Toni didn't even know yet that her mum was dead

I'll tell her later, thought Jay. *Not now.*

He didn't want anything to spoil this meeting.

Jay didn't have a comb. So he raked his hand through his springy hair, slicked it down with spit and raced out of the storeroom to find her.

He ran slap-bang into Dr Moran.

'Where's Toni?' Jay asked him.

Since Jay had first met Dr Moran, when he was searching for a cure for the plant virus, Toni's dad had always looked pale and tired, weighed down with worries. And now he had the Fungoid problem to deal with. But, even so, his appearance startled Jay. The doctor looked haunted, like a lost soul. He hardly seemed to recognise Jay at first.

Jay had a frantic thought: *What's been happening while I've been asleep?*

'I want to see Toni,' demanded Jay.

'You can't,' said Dr Moran. 'She's not here.'

Jay felt a sudden chill of dread. 'Where is she?' What have you done to her?' he shouted, right in Dr Moran's face.

'I haven't done anything to her,' said Dr Moran. 'Except tell her the truth.'

'What are you talking about?' said Jay.

'I told her about Viridian being alive. I told her that her mum was dead.'

'What did you do that for?' said Jay, appalled. 'You didn't tell her how Teal died, did you?'

'She had the right to know the truth,' said Dr Moran. 'And that means knowing everything.'

'But *I* was going to tell her,' said Jay.

'You?' Dr Moran sounded genuinely puzzled. 'I'm her father. It's my responsibility. You hardly even knew her. You only met her a few months ago.'

Jay's rage and fear spilled over. It seemed like his future was, somehow, being snatched away from him.

'I knew more about her than you did, you cold-hearted creep!' he screamed at Dr Moran. 'You told her lies. You told her she was Immune when she wasn't – '

'I shouldn't have done that,' Dr Moran acknowledged. 'And that's why I told her the truth just now. The whole truth.'

But Jay wasn't listening. His voice burned with contempt. 'You didn't even care about her. It was like, "Oh, I'm too busy saving the world to bother with one person. Even if she is my own daughter" – '

'Shut your mouth!' Dr Moran yelled at Jay.

Jay was shocked into silence. He'd never seen Dr Moran so distressed before. He'd always seemed so distant and cold, like he didn't have any human emotions.

They glared at each other while Dr Moran's face twisted as he tried to get his feelings under control.

Jay thought he was going to say something else, but he didn't. He just turned his back and strode off towards his laboratory.

Jay ran after him. 'Tell me where Toni is,' he begged. He grabbed Dr Moran's arm. 'Is she human again? I mean, I know she'll still have her wings for a bit, but...'

'Listen to me!' barked Dr Moran, swinging round. 'She doesn't want to be human again. Not ever. She wants to stay a Venus Angel. We've both lost her. Don't you understand?'

Jay's face crumpled. He felt devastated. It didn't make it any better that, deep in his mind, this was what he'd feared all along.

'Why didn't you force her to take the vaccine?' he said, wildly, hardly knowing what he was saying.

'Are you serious?' said Dr Moran. 'Are you saying that I should force her to be something she doesn't want to be?'

Jay didn't know how to answer that. His brain was swirling in confusion. 'Has she gone back to the swamplands?' he blurted out.

Even now, he was desperately clinging onto his dream. He was thinking: *If I could just see her, talk to her, I can make everything all right.*

'No,' said Dr Moran. 'She hasn't gone back there, not yet anyway. She's gone to kill Viridian.'

Jay stared at him, horrified. '*What?*'

'She's gone to get revenge, for what Viridian did to her mum. You're right, I should never have told Toni how she died. Sometimes, the whole truth is too much.'

Jay tried to imagine Toni, alone, in Viridian's underground empire. It was everything Venus Angels hated: no sunshine; no space to soar.

'How can she kill Viridian?' said Jay. 'No-one can kill him.'

'I made another mistake,' confessed Dr Moran. 'I was just trying to *talk* to Toni, as I never had time to before. I told her the ways I'd researched to kill Viridian. How there wasn't a fungicide powerful enough. Then I told her how spores can be made to explode.'

Jay tried to think back to when he was underground. He couldn't remember anything exploding. But then he couldn't remember much at all about being a zombie slave.

'It needs certain conditions,' Dr Moran was saying. 'But some kinds of dust or powder can be ignited even by a small spark. You just need the powder in high concentration, in a confined space.'

Like in Viridian's cave, Jay thought immediately.

'I told Toni nothing would survive the explosion,' Dr Moran continued. 'But that we couldn't do it because the Fungoids would die along with him, and so would whoever went down to set fire to the spores. It'd be a suicide mission.'

'She can't have gone down there.' Jay shook his head.

'When she left, she took matches from the kitchen with her,' said Dr Moran. 'What does a Venus Angel need matches for?'

'I'm going after her,' said Jay.

'*I'm* going after her, 'Dr Moran corrected him. 'And I'm going alone. All of this is my fault. I told her about her mum. I knew by then she was going to stay a Venus Angel. I thought she wouldn't be upset. I thought she'd be like every other Verdan, a loner, just caring about her own survival.'

'Toni's not like any other Verdan. She's different. She saved me from drowning.'

But Dr Moran wasn't listening to Jay. He was searching in drawers, looking for something. He pulled out a white gauze face mask.

'Is that so you don't breathe in the spores? Aren't you going to take one for Toni?' asked Jay, struggling to keep his voice steady, even though there was chaos inside his head.

'Toni won't need one,' said Dr Moran. 'The spores won't affect her. Plant-human hybrids breathe through their skin.'

'Where's Dad?' said Jay, suddenly, looking around.

Dr Moran answered Jay, as he moved quickly around the lab, searching for other stuff. 'He's in Franklin, been gone since dawn. He got a cement mixer from somewhere. He and the other citizens are filling in holes. Rather pointless, of course, because those Fungoids can tunnel up anywhere. But people like to feel useful.'

Then he strode towards a store room. It was always kept locked because it contained all kinds of dangerous chemicals.

'There are reports coming from the south,' he told Jay over his shoulder. 'There are more Venus Angels than we thought.'

Jay stared at Dr Moran, dismayed, unbelieving. 'More of them?' he whispered. 'Still alive?'

'Definitely still alive,' said Dr Moran. 'People in coastal towns have seen them flying out over the sea.'

'Where are they all going?' Jay asked Dr Moran, his heart full of foreboding.

'No-one knows,' said Dr Moran, unlocking the store room door. 'They're all flying out in the same direction. But no-one's seen them coming back.'

'You haven't told Toni yet, have you?' asked Jay urgently. 'That there are more Venus Angels?'

'No,' said Dr Moran. 'I heard about it too late, after she'd gone. But I intend to, when I find her. She doesn't want to be

119

with humans, that's obvious. She wants to be with her own kind.'

Dr Moran went into the storeroom.

Jay hesitated for about two seconds. Then he raced across the lab, and turned the key in the storeroom door. He pulled the key out and dropped it in his pocket.

'Let me out,' came Dr Moran's furious voice from inside. It was muffled because the door was thick. He wouldn't be able to break it down. There were no windows in the store room. So he wouldn't be able to escape, not until Dad came back from filling in holes.

'Let me out!' yelled Dr Moran, hammering on the door. 'I *order* you not to go after Toni!'

'Like I'm going to take any notice,' Jay murmured, as he scooped up the gauze mask and left the lab.

Outside the basement door, Jay looked around.

'It must be here somewhere,' he told himself.

He was searching for the hole where that zombie slave had come up and almost snatched Dr Moran. They'd probably blocked it off straightaway. But Jay figured if it was only with rocks, or paving stones, he might be able to shift them. It would be his quickest route down to Viridian's kingdom.

But when he found the place, Jay cursed out loud. He thought, *Why did I sleep so long?*

Hours before Jay woke up, Dad had been busy with his mixer. He'd poured cement down the hole and it was already setting.

Jay thought, *What do I do now?*

He only knew two other sure ways down to Viridian's empire. One was the old mine entrance, but that was miles out of town. The other was the Etiolation Cave.

Maybe Dad's filled that in too, thought Jay.

But it was out on the edge of Franklin, in a jungly wasteland. Maybe Dad didn't think it was top priority. And, besides, no citizens ever went near that cave, where Verdans had been punished. Many of them had dreadful memories.

Jay didn't want to go back there either. He had terrible memories too.

But he had to catch up with Toni before she found Viridian.

Did she go through the Etiolation Cave? Jay wondered. Did Toni see, for the very first time, the place where her mother Teal had died? The rock that she'd been chained to?

If she did, she'd want vengeance even more. A warrior angel, driven by human rage and grief – it was a deadly combination.

Jay started running, taking a short cut, over the fields.

CHAPTER SEVENTEEN

Toni didn't access Viridian's underground empire through the Etiolation cave. She'd gone down the hole outside the Franklin High basement just after dawn, when Jay was still sound asleep and before his dad got busy with his cement mixer.

Someone had temporarily blocked it with a giant rock. Even with a Venus Angel's superior strength, Toni had trouble shifting it. But eventually, using all her muscle power, she heaved the rock aside. With her wings folded against her back, she could just wriggle through.

At first she was slithering like a worm. It felt like she was buried alive, in darkness, with no room to spread her wings. It was a Venus Angel's worst nightmare. Only her hunger to avenge her mother drove her on.

Jay believed that Toni had been forced to become a Venus Angel. But she hadn't – she'd done it willingly. She had lost her mother once, when Teal turned Verdan then rose through the ranks to top Cultivar. And Toni had decided, *When I'm a Venus Angel, she'll notice me again*. They would be together.

Teal would be proud of her warrior angel daughter, the most perfect Verdan ever created.

But Toni didn't know then that Teal was already dead, lost to her forever, because of Viridian's treachery.

Now the narrow tunnel had opened into a wide one. Toni just enough had room to fly. She took off, her great wings brushing the tunnel walls.

She saw no Fungoids; the zombie slaves were digging elsewhere, extending Viridian's empire. But the tunnels were teeming with other fungus life. Like a speeded-up film, birth, growth, decay, the whole cycle of life was happening all around her. Fungi punched through the tunnel floor like tiny fists, blossomed into stars, sent out clouds of spores, collapsed into black slime and died. In seconds, others came up to replace them.

Luminous fungi, yellow, orange and purple, crowded the tunnel walls. They cast a glow, like stained-glass windows. Toni flew on through the colours, carefully, with slow, majestic wing flaps.

She knew Viridian was near. She could smell him. He was where decay and death were greatest.

She felt no terror at all. Her mind was focussed on one single purpose. She rattled the matchbox in the pocket of her tatty shorts.

'I am coming,' she whispered. 'And I am going to kill you.'

But Toni had no idea what she was taking on.

Viridian had his own biological surveillance system, more sophisticated than any technology. He didn't need CCTV cameras, or hidden microphones. His hyphae sampled the air. They sent back complex chemical signals, smell molecules, to where Viridian squatted in his jewelled cave. In his new Fungoid form he could interpret these messages. He knew exactly what was happening even in the furthest corners of his empire. He knew when it was under threat, how many intruders, how far away, whether they were human or Verdan. He could often tell, from their individual scent, made up of hundreds of different smell molecules, exactly who they were.

So, as soon as Toni entered his subterranean empire, Viridian's hyphae alerted him. They sent back constant updates, as fast as electricity speeds along wires, so Viridian could trace her route. He knew about every wing flap. He could even tell, from the chemicals that transpired from her body, what kind of mood she was in.

He knew she was fired up for battle. But he also knew she was one very confused Venus Angel.

He had his vast Fungoid army to defend him. But he didn't think he'd need them with this intruder.

'Come on, warrior angel,' murmured Viridian, smiling. 'I'm waiting for you.'

CHAPTER EIGHTEEN

J ay was in the wasteland on the edge of Franklin, breathless after his run, clutching his burning side, waiting for the pain to ease.

He straightened up, looked around. Things were different since he had last been here. The grass was taller. Plants had taken over, swarming everywhere, invading the derelict buildings, smashing through roofs and windows.

At first, Jay couldn't find the trapdoor that led down to the Etiolation Cave. He crashed through bracken and ferns in a frenzy, gasping, 'Where is it? Where is it?'

He even thought, *Maybe I came to the wrong place.* Maybe being a zombie slave had messed up his mind more than he thought.

Then he found the trapdoor, half-hidden, choked by brambles.

He saw immediately that Dad hadn't been here with his cement mixer.

Toni didn't come this way either, Jay thought. No one had opened that trap door for a long time.

The spiny creepers put up a fight, raking Jay's skin, as he ripped them aside. He'd expected the trapdoor beneath to be padlocked, or blocked off somehow. It wasn't, though. As if the citizens of Franklin, now they were human again, had shut this place out of their minds, pretending it never existed.

With bleeding hands, Jay yanked up the trap door. He stared into the gloom, at the slope of tumbled rocks that led to the cave floor. He felt a shivering deep in his guts. Then he took a big breath, fastened the face mask over his mouth and nose, and began to climb down.

The cave was empty, of course. He tried to ignore the rock where Teal had been chained. But, somehow, his gaze slipped towards it. There was nothing left to see, only a stain where her body had been. Jay hurried on through the flickering shadows into the tunnels beyond.

The mask was sweaty against his face. It was hard to breathe through the gauze. And the air was bad down here anyway – there was just enough for Viridian's slaves to stay alive.

Jay felt like he was suffocating. But he didn't dare remove his mask, even for a second. He could see the spores hanging like mist in the air above him. One lungful of those would be like letting Viridian in to take control of his mind.

There was massive fungus activity all around him. Earthstars growing and dying, hyphae threads snaking up through the floor, waving around as if sniffing the air.

Jay came to a T-junction. Which way now? He couldn't remember the route to Viridian's cave as well as he'd thought. He took a right turn but it was a dead end – he found himself facing a wall of rock. So he went back and tried the left-hand tunnel.

It led to the cave with the polished jet floor. Jay remembered his zombie slave captors had dragged him through here.

This is the way, thought Jay. He skidded across the jet and into the tunnel beyond.

As he approached Viridian's cave, the luminous fungi got weirder and weirder, as if they were the creations of the great tyrant's twisted mind. They made grotesque and fantastical shapes. They crawled, writhed and clustered like living creatures. They sparkled though the dark like sinister jewels.

I'm close now, thought Jay. Even through the gauze mask he could smell death and decay, growing stronger with every step he took. He wondered where Toni was.

He tried to persuade himself, *Perhaps she isn't down here at all. Perhaps she's changed her mind about avenging her mum and has flown back to the swamplands*. But he didn't really believe that.

Then he heard her voice. Another voice answered it. It was Viridian. Jay knew how that voice could change in seconds. He'd heard it low and menacing, crowing with self-belief, howling in fury from lips flecked with green foam. But now it was charming, as sweet as honey. Jay knew that was when Viridian was at his most dangerous.

'You have come to thank me,' Viridian was saying.

'I have come to kill you,' Toni answered, her voice sounding tiny in the vast, echoing cave, 'because you killed my mother, Teal.'

Jay crept up to the cave entrance. Purple fungus waved around it like sea anemones. Jay hid himself among its jelly tentacles and peeked inside.

At first he saw only Viridian, glowing corpse-white in the spore haze that puffed from his body. Thin sticky threads, millions of them, slid from his rubbery skin. They fanned out all around him, before burrowing underground. He seemed to Jay like some monstrous spider, squatting in the centre of its web. Only his head was free of hyphae. He tilted the axe-shaped crest to look down at something.

Then Jay saw Tony. Compared to the hulk towering above her she seemed as small as a dragonfly.

'You should be grateful to me,' said Viridian, making his rubbery lips into a smile. 'Because I gave you the best gift ever. I made you into a Venus Angel. You owe me.'

Jay strained to hear Toni's reply, through the twittering bats, high up in the cave roof. He thought she would say something like, 'I hate you even more for that. You made me into a freak.'

But she didn't.

'I did owe you,' Toni acknowledged. ''Cos you gave me one precious thing. But you took away another. So now I owe you *nothing*.'

Viridian ignored those last words. His voice grew even more coaxing and silky smooth. 'Come with me,' he said, his pearly eyes shining with dreams of power. 'Come with me, on the biggest adventure ever.'

Jay's heart chilled as Viridian showed a glimpse of that teenage Verdan who'd come swaggering into Dad's diner last summer.

'There should be an alliance,' continued Viridian, 'between me and the Venus Angels. Together we could rule this planet. Venus Angels above in the green world. Me below with my Fungoid slaves. What do you say?'

Toni said nothing. Far, far above, in the cave roof, bats swooped about on silent wings, diving in and out of the spore clouds.

Was Toni tempted? Jay thought, *Please Toni, don't say yes.*

Then Toni burst out, 'I don't believe you. You betrayed my mum. And, anyway, there's no other Venus Angels. I'm the only one left.'

For once Viridian, who boasted, 'I know everything,' seemed taken by surprise.

'Who told you that?' he asked Toni.

Toni said, 'Shut up. Enough talking. You're trying to mess with my brain. You killed my mother, you murdering creep, and I'm going to kill you.' She took out the matches and shook one from the box.

Quickly, Jay stepped into the cave. He pleaded, his words muffled by the mask, 'Toni, don't strike that match.'

Viridian said, 'Welcome. I wondered when you would show yourself.'

'Go away,' Toni told Jay. 'This is nothing to do with you.'

'There'll be a fire, a big explosion. You'll die along with him.'

Toni didn't answer. She flew upwards on fluttering wings holding the box in one hand, the match in the other. Both her hands were rock steady.

'Run,' she told Jay.

At that moment, one of Viridian's hyphae, sniffing the air around Toni, sent him a complex chemical message. Viridian analysed that message in a split second, and thought, amazed, *She will do it! She still loves her mother!*

Viridian finally realised he'd made a rare mistake. Venus Angels weren't the perfect Verdans he'd hoped for. They were flawed, polluted by messy human emotions.

He hadn't, in any case, been planning an alliance with them. He'd meant to dazzle Toni with his dreams, trick her into leading the other Venus Angels right into his trap, then kill them all. Viridian didn't believe in power-sharing. He always ruthlessly terminated rivals.

But, in an instant, he re-arranged his plans.

Viridian's Fungoid body started to self-destruct, as fast as his Earthstars in the tunnels. He seemed to explode glittering spores, from his skin, mouth, nose and eyes. His glowing white flesh grew darker, began to decay. As Jay stared upwards, horrified, the great mutant seemed to collapse into himself from the top down. First that warlike crest curled and melted. Then his features grew blurry and his whole face melted into the black jelly mess that had once been his head.

'Toni!' Jay cried out. But Toni was lost somewhere up in the smoky spore clouds.

Jay crouched down, hid behind a rock and held his mask on tight. The stench of decay was choking him.

At last, after what seemed like ages, Jay dared to raise his head, just a little. He saw a bare green foot, with freshly healed wounds.

Toni had fluttered down and landed beside him. He gazed up at her. The box and the unlit match were dangling from her hands. She seemed to have forgotten all about them.

'Toni, you OK?' Jay asked her anxiously.

But she wasn't looking at him, wasn't even listening. Jay peered over the rock, so he could see what she was staring at. The spore clouds seemed to be settling. Luminous fungi on the cave walls cast a purple glow over the whole grotesque scene.

Viridian was a mountain of collapsed fungoid flesh. Slime was sliding down its slopes and spreading over the cave floor in black oily pools.

'What's happened to him?' whispered Jay, appalled.

But he already knew the answer. Viridian had decomposed, like his Earthstars. His hyphae, going into the cave floor, had all withered and rotted too.

Jay went closer, side-stepping a slime tide that was creeping closer to his shoes.

'No!' Toni grabbed his arm. 'Keep away. Don't touch it.'

She was shivering. She couldn't take her eyes off what had once been Viridian.

'It's OK,' said Jay. 'He's dead. He's really dead.' As relief surged through him in crashing waves, he started crying with laughter, in great, gulping whoops through the mask. He sounded hysterical. But he couldn't help himself.

'He said, "I am Immortal",' Toni was murmuring, shaking her head, as if she still couldn't believe what she saw.

At last, Jay hiccupped himself to a stop. He wiped tears from his stinging eyes. His laughing fit had left him as weak as a new-born kitten. He had to sit down on the rock because his legs felt so shaky.

'He told me that too,' he said when he was finally able to speak. 'But he isn't immortal, is he? I mean, look at him. He's just a pile of gloop. You should be celebrating. That's what you wanted, isn't it?'

'I want to get out of this place,' said Toni.

She flew upwards again, 'There's a way out up here,' she called down.

'Where?' said Jay.

'Where the bats get in,' said Toni. 'I'll meet you outside.'

'Wait!' said Jay. But her body, supple as a plant creeper, was sliding through a gap in the roof Jay hadn't even noticed before. And he was alone in the cave.

Jay took one last glance at what was left of Viridian. Then he took off, running back the way he'd come in. He skidded about in the squelchy mess on the tunnel floors. All the Earthstars were decomposing and, with Viridian dead, no new ones were pushing up in their place. It seemed that the great tyrant's underground Empire, like his body, was in ruins.

As Jay hurried back through the Etiolation Cave, his mind was racing, along with his heart. He didn't glance once at the place where Teal's body had been. He wasn't thinking about the past any more. He was thinking hard, about what lay ahead for him and Toni.

Now he was out in the bright morning, blinking after the dark tunnels. And to his surprise there was Toni, perched on the roof of a derelict building, flexing her beautiful wings. He'd half-expected her not to be waiting.

But she fluttered down beside him.

'Why did you come after me?' she asked him curiously.

'I was scared you were going to blow yourself up, along with Viridian.'

Toni stared at him as if he was a stranger, as if he didn't understand the slightest thing about her. 'I'm the last Venus Angel,' she told him with fierce pride. 'It's my duty to stay alive.'

Already, her green eyes, filled with sunshine, were turned skywards, as if she was picturing herself, up there flying. Jay knew she was frantic to get away.

A deep sadness gripped him. There was no future for him and Toni. He'd been lying to himself over and over. Even when he heard her just now agreeing that Viridian gave her the best gift ever when he'd made her a Venus Angel.

'Look, it's not going to work is it, you and me?' he burst out. 'I was sure that you'd want to be human again. But I got it all wrong.'

Toni was tired of speaking English; it felt such a clumsy way to communicate. But she made one more effort. 'Jay, if I was human...'

Jay said, defensively, 'It's OK, you don't have to make me feel better. I'll get over it.'

Toni fixed him with those glittering, predator's eyes. She finished what she was saying, 'If I was human,' she said, 'I would choose you.'

And that was the last English Jay ever heard her speak.

But there was one last thing he needed to tell her. It was something he'd been going to keep secret, if there'd been any chance at all that she'd take the vaccine. But that was never going to happen.

'You're not the last Venus Angel,' Jay told her. 'There are more like you. People have seen them, down in the south, flying out to sea. And they're going someplace, because they haven't been coming back.'

Toni stared at him.

'It's true,' said Jay, his voice calmer and more steady than he felt. 'So you should go and find them.'

Toni hesitated for a minute. Then her wings began beating. She streaked into the sky like an arrow let loose, heading, it seemed, straight for the sun. Then she stopped dead, hovering high up on outspread wings, scanning the landscape spread out before her.

Did she glance back at him? Jay could never be sure about that. She started flying again, heading South with strong, powerful wing flaps and disappeared over a row of tall pine trees.

For a long time after she'd gone, Jay kept staring into the sky, shading his eyes against the sun. Then he gave up and began trudging back home.

It was a relief in a way that it was all over. No more pretending; no more hopeless hoping. So why did he feel so hollow inside, like something amazing and magical had been ripped from his life?

When Jay reached the Franklin High basement, Dad still wasn't back. Jay was looking for something to eat in the kitchen when Dr Moran came in.

Jay didn't have the energy to pick a fight. But he wasn't going to tell Dr Moran he'd been right all along either.

Instead he said, 'Toni's safe. I told her about the other Venus Angels. She's gone to find them.'

Dr Moran nodded. Jay waited for a flood of questions. But Dr Moran just said, 'Is she happy?'

'Yes,' said Jay.

'That's good,' said Dr Moran. 'That's all I wanted.'

Jay had intended to be tight-lipped, but somehow it all came pouring out. He told Dr Moran what had happened down in the cave, how Viridian had suddenly dissolved into slime.

'So he's dead, right?' said Jay.

Dr Moran didn't seem to hear that question. 'Fascinating,' he breathed, back in scientist mode again. 'I'll explain. Fungi have this amazing ability. They produce enzymes that break down their own cells. Basically they rot themselves. I think Viridian chose to do the same.'

'Wait a minute,' said Jay, putting down the hunk of bread he'd been wolfing, staring at Dr Moran. 'What do you mean, *chose*? I thought we were just lucky – that he died when he did, just before Toni was going to strike that match.'

'I don't think luck had anything to do with it,' said Dr Moran.

Jay repeated his question. 'He is dead, isn't he?'

But Dr Moran was already on his way back to his laboratory. So Jay didn't hear him murmuring, 'That depends…'

CHAPTER NINETEEN

Jay was eating cold baked beans straight from the can when Dad came into the kitchen and slumped down in a chair.

'Want some?' Jay said, pushing the can and spoon across the table.

Dad shook his head. 'I'm not hungry.'

He looked shattered, his clothes covered in crusty, dried cement. Then he started crying, tears streaming down his face.

Jay stared, astonished. He'd seen Dad angry and upset sometimes. But he'd never, ever seen him cry before. Jay didn't know the right words to say in this situation. So he just blurted out, clumsily, 'What's up, Dad?'

Dad buried his head in his hands, rocked for a while, then looked up again, his face still streaked with tears. Finally he said, 'I'm sorry, son.'

'About what?' asked Jay, bewildered.

'About what happened with Toni. Dr Moran just told me everything. That you lost her.'

And now Dad's shoulders were heaving again. He was biting his lip but still sobbing like a baby, for Jay's broken dreams, for lost loves.

'I'm sorry it turned out that way,' said Dad, voice choked.

Suddenly Jay knew what to do. It just seemed to come naturally. He scraped his chair back, went around the table and, like a parent comforting a sad child, he put his arm around Dad's shoulders. It seemed to Jay, at that moment, that he was the older, wiser one.

'It's OK, Dad,' Jay reassured him. 'It's OK. I'll be all right, honest.'

Dad wiped his running nose with the back of his hand. 'You mean that? I thought you'd be…'

Jay interrupted. 'I'll be all right,' he repeated, firmly. 'It couldn't have worked out, could it? Once I knew she wouldn't turn human. I mean, me and a Venus Angel? Get real.'

'Maybe she'll change her mind…' began Dad.

But Jay didn't want to go there. He didn't want to cause himself any more useless pain.

'Forget it, Dad,' said Jay. 'She won't ever go back to being human. She'd die first.'

There was silence between them for a minute. Then, sounding much cheerier, Dad said, 'So what now? What do you want to do with the rest of your life? Say I found a new trailer? We could live there, like we did before. Start up the old business again: Rainbirds American Diner.'

'I don't know,' said Jay.

'I thought you'd like that,' said Dad, disappointed. 'You wouldn't just be flipping burgers. You could be my business partner.' He frowned. 'But maybe you should go back to school. Maybe you should do that.'

'I don't know,' Jay repeated. And he really didn't. It was too soon. He'd only just got used to the idea of a future without Toni. The one thing he did know was that he felt like a different person to the boy he'd been before.

'I'll think about it,' Jay promised Dad. 'About what I want to do with the rest of my life. And when I know, I'll get back to you.'

Toni had left the south coast far behind. She was travelling over the ocean. She was hungry. Suddenly, like a diving seabird, she folded her wings and plunged headfirst into the waves. Her green skin glittered with oxygen bubbles as she seemed to fly through water, like a great manta ray. She caught a fish in her spiny wings. Her ancillary wings, beating fast, brought her shooting out of the ocean in a fountain of rainbow spray.

Up in the sky again, Toni laughed out loud. It was the first time she'd ever tried hunting underwater. Being a Venus Angel had opened up whole new worlds.

She hovered while she digested the fish. Then she was off again, swooping over the wave crests, searching for the rest of her species.

Night came but Toni didn't rest. She flew on through the rain and dark. When dawn came it had stopped raining. But she couldn't fly any further. She looked around for somewhere to land.

Then rising out of the mist she saw an island. Taking off from its mountains she saw Venus Angels, perhaps two hundred of them, created in laboratories all over the world before the Verdan dream turned sour. They flew out through the fiery dawn sky to welcome her.

None of them spoke. They didn't need to. They just surrounded Toni, for support, in case her weary wings gave way. And they escorted her to her new home.

CHAPTER TWENTY

Back in the jewelled cave, nothing happened for a long time. The rotting heap, all that remained of Viridian, stayed just as Jay and Toni had left it.

As day turned to dusk, the bats grew more active, swooping around high in the roof, exercising their wings. Some bats flew lower than others. They brushed the top of the slime mountain where Viridian's brain had been. A few spores stuck to their furry bodies and when they flew out of the cave, into the night air, they carried the spores with them.

As they darted about, hunting moths, a few of Viridian's spores got detached and drifted away, up into the atmosphere. Most spores never escape the earth's gravitational pull. And, if they do, they often die. Viridian's spores were supreme survivors but still, only a few of them made it. They attached themselves to rock fragments and went whirling off into deep space among fiery-tailed comets, and meteor showers.

A spore found a planet that could support its life. It was one of the many moons of Jupiter in the Milky Way. It was also honeycombed with caves under its surface. The spore landed in a fissure and slipped down into the darkness of the cave system. Immediately, it sent out hyphae that began drilling back upwards.

On the planet's surface, a fairy ring of what seemed like giant fungi appeared. The first sign of them was a circle of seven pleated crests that came slicing up like axe blades. They were attached to slippery smooth domes, like the caps of the deadly Destroying Angel. But, as the domes swelled and pushed up further, features became visible. On each of them, fierce, pale eyes shot open and stared around. Viridian was cloning himself.

The white scaly lips appeared. And the first words they chanted, in unison, were 'We are Immortal.'

Viridian had meant to conquer Earth first, then spread out throughout the Universe. But this slight change of plan didn't matter. Earth was such a small, insignificant scrap of rock anyway. It was hardly worth including in his Empire. But if the human race thought it had escaped, it hadn't.

Sooner or later, because of global warming, much of the Earth would be desert. Humans would be forced to find other planets to live on. Viridian couldn't wait to see their faces, when the first colonists landed here, thinking they'd found a safe haven.

And if they didn't choose this planet, that didn't matter either. Because by then every habitable planet within easy reach of Earth would be ruled by Viridians.

'Welcome,' the Viridians would say, as the first humans poured, eager and hopeful, from their spaceships after their long voyage. 'We've been waiting for you.'